MYTHICAL SUNSHINE

SHUBORNO CHAKROBORTY

I dedicate this story:

To the one who gave me sweet memories and sleepless nights,

To the one who pushed me to the never ending thoughts of agony and despair,

To the one who made me ponder about my creative madness,

To the one who rests above the clouds,

To the one who resides within my soul.

Contents

Contents

Preface

In July 2024, I traveled to Bangladesh for a teaching assignment at the Asian University for Women in Chittagong. Midway through the month, a wave of civil unrest swept the streets. Tragically, some students lost their lives, and videos of these horrifying moments went viral, igniting fierce debates across the internet. The Bangladeshi government imposed an internet blackout, severely disrupting telecommunication channels. International calls became nearly impossible, and I couldn't reach my family in India, who were deeply concerned about my well-being. Additionally, I was dealing with personal issues, and my emotions were on a roller coaster. For seven excruciating days, there was no internet. The first two days were torturous, but by the third day, a sense of peace began to settle within me. Surprisingly, without the internet, my mental and emotional well-being started to improve.

My colleagues, who were staying in the same building, became more social, and our evenings were filled with conversations without the distraction of phones. Incessant browsing through Facebook and Instagram ceased, and the irritating notifications from Snapchat fell silent. Digital communication practically vanished, leaving room for genuine human interaction. This experience led me to ponder the darker aspects of technology, particularly how it has intertwined itself with our daily lives, influencing our emotions and behaviors.

In the early 1990s, air conditioners were not common in our homes. Power cuts, which were routine during summer evenings, were something we genuinely looked forward to. Thirst could be quenched with water from an earthen pot; there was no need for ice-cold water. Evenings were spent playing outdoor sports, and real communication happened face to face. Long-distance relationships often thrived because people were patient, and the demand for immediacy had not yet overtaken us. However, in the last 25 years, technology has advanced rapidly. Faster and instant communication, social networking, and easy access to the internet have made our lives much more convenient. On the other hand, these advancements may have negatively affected our morals, ethics, integrity, and even character. Here, my use of the term "technology" is broad but slightly skewed towards the internet, digital communication, and artificial intelligence.

A critical aspect of the history of technology is its connection to humanity's ongoing pursuit of reducing physical and mental toil. Technology has catapulted humankind to new heights, leading to discoveries and inventions that have made life easier and more efficient. It is the human need to explore the unknown that drives us, with the help of technology, not only to traverse the vast expanses of the sky but also to probe the mysteries of the human body and the universe. It has transformed communication and transportation, bringing nations and people closer together, creating a global network. It has enriched economies and improved lifestyles, making it increasingly possible to connect with anyone, anywhere, at any time.

The pursuit of minimizing physical and mental exertion gave birth to the computer age, gradually paving the way for robotics and automation As technological evolution accelerated, it became increasingly intertwined with society, revealing several areas of concern. Carbon emissions increased, contributing to global warming and raising alarms about climate change. The development of dangerous weapons, including nuclear bombs, posed new threats. The endless desire for power, control, and domination grew exponentially. Technological advancements began to profoundly influence human behavior and thought processes.

It is on this premise that I considered the dual-edged nature of technological development in this novella. The same forces that have united us and elevated us to unprecedented heights also have the potential to tear us apart. The future of our species depends on our ability to balance these competing dynamics, embracing the power of technology while remaining deeply aware of its impact on our emotions, actions, and the world around us.

Many of our problems stem from our unregulated emotions. Achieving a state of well-balanced emotional health is, in itself, a challenging task. Now, imagine a world where sentient AI robots are engineered with emotions. Would that be a boon for them or for the world in general? More importantly, would it benefit humanity? Would it even be possible to coexist with such advanced technological creatures? A sentient AI robot suffering from emotional issues would blur the line between them and humans. The only difference would be their capabilities. But the thought of a highly capable, powerful, yet emotional AI robot raises concerns about its impact on its surroundings. Should we assume that a highly capable sentient AI robot would have a better ability to regulate emotions than we do?

The fusion between man and machine has always captured the attention of artists, philosophers, and scientists alike, sparking debates and inspiring science fiction. Again, the question arises: if such a fusion, commonly known as cyborgs, becomes a reality and they are infused with emotions, what would be the impact on them and society? Moreover, if a dictator were to upgrade humans into cyborgs to enhance our capabilities for the betterment of the world—a seemingly good idea—would that be ethically and morally appropriate? And even if it were done, how would emotions affect them? Would it be better to completely eliminate emotions from cyborgs?

Our penchant for playing the role of God has led to the rise of artificial intelligence. For the last few decades, we have been striving to create something that surpasses human capabilities, and this pursuit is rapidly growing. Perhaps it is a reflection of technology's impact, particularly AI, on our lives that led me to imagine a future where technological evolution has reached its zenith, along with our insatiable thirst for power.

Through this story, I aim to provoke thought and reflection on the ethical and moral issues surrounding artificial intelligence, the reciprocal impact of technology on society, and the crucial role of emotional well-being in our lives. Most importantly, I invite the readers to think about the possibility of a cyborg or AI with emotions and the profound implications such an existence would have on our society.

Acknowledgements

To my loving family, especially my elder brother, Mr. Shubham Chakraborty:

You have remained by my side through my highs and lows, offering solace during moments of doubt and celebrating every milestone with unbridled joy. Your unwavering faith in my abilities has fueled my determination to pursue my dreams and push the boundaries of my creativity.

To my teachers at the Indian Institute of Technology (IIT), New Delhi and Centre for Behavioral and Cognitive Sciences (CBCS), Allahabad:

Thank you for enlightening me about the intricate connection between technology and society and instilling in me an enduring enthusiasm for understanding the human mind. My four years spent in both of these institutes of excellence and eminence have given me a new direction to showcase my creativity and storytelling prowess.

To my experiences:

You have been the reason behind the highs and lows in my life. Your majestic ways of testing my limits through the fire of emotional turmoil and seemingly hopeless situations has helped me make a comeback each time with greater wisdom and learning than before. I eagerly await more such trials.

To my emotional vulnerabilities, my impulsivity, my overthinking mind, my fickle-mindedness, my unconventional career, my loneliness, my mood swings, and most importantly, my genes:

This novella wouldn't have been possible without the perfect balance of all these.

Prologue

It was the year 2199, and the world was on the verge of a new era. The lines between humans and machines were nearly dissolved. The world was almost completely overtaken by artificial general intelligence and cybernetic organisms. These were no longer part of science fiction or topics of intense debate.

The planet Earth, renamed Queen's Paradise, was ruled by a phenomenal creature—the Queen, a supremely powerful cyborg, a symbiotic amalgamation of human consciousness and machine intelligence. She was the product of centuries of technological evolution and the unparalleled effort of human creativity. She had reached the pinnacle of power, but with great power came incredible perils.

As the world approached the year 2200, Queen's Paradise was hit by a virus that did not contaminate the body but the minds of the cybernetic organisms—or cyborgs—designed by the Queen herself. The entire community of cyborgs faced an unprecedented challenge.

But in this fully mechanized world, there was only one human who stood like a rock against this technological domination, clinging to the very core of humanity—the Professor. He was creating a roadblock against the rise of the cyborg community by holding on to something essential to save the human race.

Would the Professor be able to restore the essence of humanity? Or would it mark the beginning of a newfound "peace," devoid of any human folly, beneficial for the planet Earth—Queen's Paradise?

CHAPTER ONE

THE RESEARCHER

- **Year:** 2145
- **Location:** School of Artificial General Intelligence, College of Engineering, New Delhi

"Since time immemorial, humans have dreamed of a world beyond their grasp. In the last few centuries, those dreams have evolved into patterns of zeros and ones. Now, humans are steering ahead, taking another leap in their greatest quest ever: the creation of artificial general intelligence (AGI). As you all know, artificial intelligence (AI) technologies function within a set of predetermined parameters. For example, AI models trained in image recognition and generation are unable to build websites. AGI is the pursuit of developing AI systems that possess autonomous self-control, a reasonable degree of self-understanding, and the ability to learn new skills. AGI would solve complex problems in various settings and contexts without requiring prior training," said the AI-created imaginary human, known as the AI tutor, while teaching a class full of students. It moved from one bluish glass screen to another, scattered across the classroom, while delivering its first lecture on the introduction to general artificial intelligence.

"Humans have always had a tendency to play the role of creator. Over time, they have improved through learning and feedback. With each invention, from the simplest algorithms to the complexity of today's neural networks, the ultimate goal of human technological prowess will be the creation of machine consciousness—a machine that will have subjective conscious experience, sentience, and a mind. This could happen anytime soon, given the rate at which technology has undergone massive evolution in the last few hundred years. I believe that once AGI is ready, it won't take long to unleash machine consciousness as well. Though utilizing AGI to upgrade human abilities to create a cyborg—an intriguing mix of man and machine—remains a theoretical concept and research goal, within the next twenty-five to thirty years, it may become a reality. We may all witness a cyborg in our lifetimes," said the AI tutor as students looked around, surprise in their eyes.

The AI tutor continued, "Yet, in all this pursuit, there is something deeper: the desire to transcend and go beyond human cognitive and physical limitations. In AGI, humans seek a companion, a coworker who would collaborate with them in their quest to solve the mysteries of life and the universe. But as technology stands on the brink of creating minds that will surpass human limitations, this search is also a step into the unknown, where every step is juxtaposed with questions of ethics, control, agency, and even the nature of existence itself."

In the last one hundred twenty-five years, technology around large language models has taken exponential strides to reach this stage. It all began with simple chatbots and virtual assistants. The technology advanced every year, and by the end of the twenty-first century, AI technologies were governing the world, initially replacing jobs in the market. The global scenario went from bad to worse; nations fought among themselves to achieve AI supremacy, understanding the importance of AI in controlling defense systems. A mini world war took place in the year 2100, primarily fought by AI robots, more or less controlled by humans. However, this resulted in extreme financial crises worldwide. Third-world countries, financially dependent on well-developed nations, felt the heat along with the severe impact of global warming. Apex bodies regulating world politics decided to create new policies and rules for nations using AI in defense systems. They also put a stop to using AI for skilled jobs that demanded repetition. All this was done to bring the world back from a technological disaster. Universities worldwide were mandated to research the ethical use of AI and the creation of AI that would only supplement humans in working toward the sustainable development of societies across the globe.

The first thing researchers brought into existence was "dynamic AI-based holographic mentors: AI tutors," which would act as teaching assistants. Initially, everyone thought they would replace professors and teachers, but after the disastrous turn of events, governments across nations enacted strict policies on the use of AI tutors. These AI tutors would look like a normal human designed by the professors teaching the courses. Every lecture hall was redesigned with bluish screens around the walls where the AI tutor would move, interacting with students in real-time and taking their questions. Only the professors were given control over how the AI tutor would look and the language they would use in class. Initially, when this technology was introduced and when control wasn't strong, students engaged in all sorts of mischievous acts, sometimes creating a bikini model with a Russian accent as an AI tutor. This led to numerous controversies, but the governments, serious this time, managed to control the situation while efficiently using new-age technology with caution. Human creativity and the madness for attaining unlimited power knew no bounds. As nations enforced strict laws, groups around the world emerged to unleash the dark side of this technology.

"But, Professor, don't you think that AI surpassing humans could create a crisis similar to—or even worse than—what we all faced forty-five years ago?" asked Shaurya Chatterjee, a research scholar studying AGI at the university. Shaurya was a tall man with handsome features. His neatly trimmed beard, rimless spectacles, and sharp nose added a dash of maturity to his boyish looks. However, he was a paradox—a handsome man with a severe case of impostor syndrome, who had no idea just how amazing he really was, both inside and out. A very kind and helpful person, he was the class topper, and the professors loved him. He came from a humble background, and through his intellectual abilities, he paved his own way into one of the premier institutions in the country. His thirst for knowledge was unending, and everyone spoke his name with admiration. Despite all this, he was a man of few words, especially around women. His natural shyness, coupled with a romantic heart, created a tense polarity between his heart and mind.

"Oh, come on, young man. First of all, don't call me 'Professor.' Your actual professor specifically instructed me to tell you this. He worries I will take his job in the future," said the AI tutor with a sheepish grin as he transformed his tuxedo into a colorful shirt and a hat, as if getting ready for the beach. The entire class giggled as they saw a sign on the screen: "Humor feedback updated." The AI tutor glanced at the update. "Well, this is the 'understanding humor' algorithm your professor fed me. But yes, getting back to your question of risks to humanity by AI, again." The AI tutor lowered his spectacles and smirked at the entire classroom. The students laughed, and another sign appeared on the screen: "Humor feedback updated." "Well, AI did try to surpass humans once, and as you all know, the world faced severe problems after that. But I think the regulations and technological control are now so tight that nothing of that sort would happen. Most importantly, the present AI is still far behind in integrating with human emotions and creativity. Perhaps the day that happens, the day 'we' understand how to control human emotions and creativity... Oh sorry, I shouldn't have used the word 'we.'" The students now laughed out loud, except for Shaurya, who was lost in his thoughts—a deep, unsettling thought was bugging him.

"Humor feedback updated."

The lecture ended, and the screens turned blue as the AI mentor went to sleep. Shaurya lifted his notebook and walked out of the classroom, murmuring to himself. A notification beeped on his smartphone: "Event: Seminar Hall: Dramatic Society: Maya Chandrasekharan." He frantically called one of his friends to lend him his cycle and started pedaling as fast as he could. He could miss anything but a glimpse of Maya, his college crush, which he could never afford to miss. She was the only possible hope to bring some sunshine to his dry, studious life.

CHAPTER TWO

THE CREATOR

- Year: 2199
- Location: Merge AI Headquarters, Queens' Paradise

Initially, AGI was humanity's greatest technological marvel. People all over the world were captivated by observing machines that could learn, think, and evolve. It was nothing less than a supernatural phenomenon. These machines were designed to solve various problems and challenges faced by humanity. But as they grew smarter and more capable, something changed. Humanity has always been plagued by power and corruption. The idea of complete control over the world has tempted many since ancient times, and it was no different with AGI. There were those who wanted to blur the lines between creator and creation permanently.

The period from 2160 to 2175 was one of the most interesting yet dangerous periods for human civilization. Technological advancement took a perilous turn when some powerful and corrupt agencies across the world decided to take a leap of faith, deceiving all the regulations sanctioned by international bodies. They did the unthinkable—they used the first-ever cyborg, an upgrade of a human into a machine, for their corrupt intentions. Instead of inventing sentient AGI, they enhanced the already sentient being into a new species that had the ability to evolve exponentially compared to humans. The entire research on the cyborgs' inception was conducted using AGI and the most advanced technological and scientific research.

The fear and suspicion regarding the development of cyborgs had always existed, but the majority of researchers across the world kept arguing that it wasn't possible. Gradually, the cyborgs acquired the ability to control the human mind and began exploiting the nine basic emotions: joy, fear, anger, love, courage, sadness, amazement, disgust, and peace. They started to upgrade humans into machines. The most basic modification they made was stripping emotions and certain memories away from humans, then making necessary changes to their brains and entire bodies. Every new cyborg was fed only one command: to gain control and supersede human civilization. Most of their memories regarding their previous identities were removed, except for their procedural memories, which aided the performance of particular tasks without conscious awareness of previous experiences. A doctor, for example, would remember all their medical skills but have no memory of whom they treated. The same was done with soldiers, researchers, and every other skilled worker. The artists and writers were all killed. Anyone who had more control over their emotions also lost their lives. Ironically, those who sought control over the world were ultimately controlled by the cyborgs.

Once the cyborgs began rising in number, they started to manipulate human minds, causing civil wars and unrest across the globe. Communal wars became rampant. Initially, governments attempted to use political and social power against them, but all the world's leaders were assassinated simultaneously, irrespective of time zones. They all committed suicide as these new beings took over their minds. The cyborgs established a company called Merge AI and renamed the planet Earth "Queens' Paradise." Merge AI's primary motive was to upgrade every human on the planet along with all the technologies present on Earth. From communication networks to airplanes to even household items, everything was upgraded to meet the needs of the cyborgs. But the one holding all the power was the strongest cyborg on the planet—the Queen, the mass producer of this new enhanced mix between humans and machines, and the head of Merge AI.

However, there was a small catch. The human creators of the cyborgs told the Queen before being killed by her that all humans on the planet must be upgraded to cyborgs by the end of 2199, within a span of twenty-five years from 2175, or else the cyborgs would gradually regain control of their emotions and other cognitive abilities. So the Queen ordered a complete stoppage of human births after the year 2185. The planet didn't see any human births for fourteen years. The twenty-five-year deadline was maintained for the first twenty-four years, but in the last year, they struggled to upgrade the last human on the planet—the Professor. An old man, he became the biggest hurdle for Merge AI, and especially for the Queen. The Merge AI cyborg researchers were going crazy, as none of their new technology worked on the Professor. They tried every possible enhancement procedure, but the old man was unshakable. Time was slowly running out; doomsday for Merge AI was near, but they simply couldn't find a solution to this problem. From brain scans to network mapping of the mind, they did everything to find the loophole. They even upgraded their own technology fifty times in six months, but something was amiss. The Queen demanded an immediate solution to this problem before time ran out.

The Professor was kept in confinement; he was an octogenarian. He remained quiet most of the day, his only companion being one cyborg who had been a healthcare worker. The human researchers who created this technology were inspired by ant colonies. The Queen AI, the ancient one, was connected to every single cyborg redesigned in her image. The researchers attempted to play the role of God, following the belief that God made man in His own image. However, this time, the cyborgs killed their own creator and now struggled to eliminate the last one left. The Professor would wake up early each morning and go for a stroll just outside his confinement. Artificially designed trees, mimicking natural ones, were invented to meet human needs and control carbon emissions. These trees emitted excess oxygen and regulated the surrounding temperature. Despite their synthetic origin, the Professor often found solace in their shade, a brief escape from the relentless scrutiny of his captors. After breakfast, he was subjected to various procedures and tests throughout the day. Each process was designed to unlock the secrets of his resistance, to understand why he, alone among millions, had not succumbed to the upgrades.

Every evening, he was taken to the "scanning chamber," a coffin-like arrangement made of platinum with a convertible glass top. A pillow was placed at the head of the chamber to cover the Professor's head, collecting data. The merger machine remained unused until the scanning chamber completed its scan and gave the green signal.

Despite being replaced thousands of times, the scanning chamber yielded no difference. The researchers in Merge AI realized there was a gap between the data they collected and the Professor's memory. The data never matched his overall memory events, and they had no idea what was missing. The issue was that until the go signal emanated from the scanning chamber, the memory deletion process could not begin. The Professor was aware of this shortcoming. He safeguarded a precious secret in his mind to prevent himself from being upgraded. Every probe had failed to extract it. He was fighting a quiet battle against this technological insanity. Time was running out, and with it, the certainty of the cyborgs' dominance over human civilization.

CHAPTER THREE

THE ARTIST

The stage was set for the upcoming drama, and the audience eagerly waited for the play to begin, directed by the campus crush of every man, Maya Chandrasekharan. A beautiful young lady with curly hair and a peachy, glowing face, her smile could even revive the lifeless. She was an undergraduate design student with an intense artistic fervor and was the head of the college's dramatic society. Maya was an exceptional person with amazing communication skills, a humble yet bold personality. Her attire was the daily topic of campus discussions. She could wear both Western and Indian clothing with equal grace. Some days, she would wear hot pants with a tank top, and men wouldn't stop thinking about her for the entire day. Other days, she would wear a simple kurta and jeans with a little bindi on her forehead, and men would hover around her like lovelorn puppies. Her hooped earrings and nose ring, paired with nude lipstick, would make guys fall for her instantly. The most interesting thing about her was the choice of perfume she wore—she would smell like a beautiful flower when she was around. She was nothing less than poetry in motion. Her movements matched the steps of a Kathak dancer, and her voice would raise dopamine levels. An epitome of art and design, her creative acts and plays were becoming increasingly popular. She was always surrounded by men—some getting friend-zoned without it being her fault, some trying to get six-pack abs to attract her, and some trying to sell all their stocks and shares to take her out to dinner. Yet, here she was: an absolute modernist on the outside but a lover of tradition and culture on the inside.

At the same time, she was bad-mouthed; rejected men would assassinate her character, coming up with different stories about her. She had faced this her entire life, and it was nothing new when she entered college. She was also vocal about the dark side of AGI, and her recent performances focused on how AGI could be a danger to society and why it must be completely stopped to return to traditional technological ways. Audiences were enthralled by her performances and the plays directed by her. On that day, the audience eagerly awaited the play written and directed by her, 'AGI: A Curse for Humanity'. The humanities department adored her, while the technology departments detested her. She was slowly transforming into the voice of the campus, an anti-AGI activist. She became the regular topic of debates across the campus, and her popularity began to rise even outside the campus. Earlier that year, she and her team were invited by the President of India to perform at the President's House in the heart of New Delhi. She received much critical acclaim, as well as a signed memento from the President. The play was telecasted all over the country, and the media went gaga over her. Amidst all this attention, she remained absolutely unfazed, even a little unhappy with the media for projecting her as a national crush, the most beautiful person in the country. She even received a few offers from filmmakers, but she rejected them. Her only condition was that she would not only act but also direct the film, and the film would be a social commentary on the dark side of AGI. She was so dedicated to her craft that all this temporary attention toward her beautiful face and voluptuous figure didn't attract her. Every day, her friends on campus advised her to become a content creator by showcasing her moves and lovely face, but her ethics wouldn't allow her to do that.

As soon as the play ended, the audience gave a standing ovation. Shaurya arrived late but entered just as everyone was clapping. He looked around at the crowd and joined in, clapping along with them. He was frustrated with himself for missing the show, but at the end of the day, it was Maya, not the play, who drew him there. He mustered up some courage to talk to her, but his shyness, anxieties, and heavily beating heart kept holding him back. On top of that, his overthinking would trigger a barrage of negative and sad thoughts whenever he saw her roaming around campus with some other guy.

When the audience started moving out, he quickly went backstage to catch a glimpse of her. He had spent the entire night preparing his first line, and when he learned that the play was about AGI, his excitement skyrocketed—finally, there was something he could talk to her about. He had no idea, though, how much she despised AGI researchers. When he reached backstage, he couldn't find anyone. He cursed himself repeatedly. Feeling dejected, he stepped out, contemplating getting some coffee, but his overthinking was eating him alive. He started imagining that she had gone on a date with the lead actor of the play after it was over.

Shaurya was a humble human being with so much groundedness that he would never accept compliments about his looks. He dressed shabbily, with no real sense of what looked good on him, making him a polar opposite of Maya when it came to aesthetic appeal. The moment he entered the Café Coffee Day (CCD), his heart skipped a beat. There, sitting right in front of him, alone inside the CCD, was Maya, working on her laptop. The CCD on campus was run by AI robots. Coffee was served by the robots, but Maya, being Maya, would go directly to the machine and prepare her own coffee, while Shaurya was fascinated every time a robot came to greet him.

Shaurya's heart was racing, his pulse far beyond normal. He stood there, staring at Maya, while internally berating himself, "Idiot, you're staring at her! What would she think?" But he couldn't tear his eyes away, as if he were paralyzed. When Maya finally lifted her head, he awkwardly turned toward the counter. His thoughts were jumbled, and he simply grabbed a glass, fixating on the robot. He was speechless. Before he could turn back to Maya, the robot spoke, "Dear Sir, I am at your service. Please take a seat and place your order from there." He took a few steps back, stood in front of Maya, and remained silent, his forehead dripping with sweat. Maya looked at him with a surprised expression.

"Yes?"

"Hi, can I sit here?"

Maya glanced around at the empty seats. Before she could respond, Shaurya realized his blunder.

"Your performance was really good today," Shaurya said, his nervousness causing him to stammer over the word "performance."

Maya gestured for him to sit across from her. As Shaurya pulled out the chair, his heavy bag slipped off his shoulder and fell to the floor. "Sorry, sorry, oh God..." he muttered, and when he bent down to pick it up, his phone slid out of his shirt pocket. His embarrassment knew no bounds. His nervousness had completely taken over. Maya watched the scene unfold, confused by what was happening in front of her. "Easy, easy, take your seat. Do you need some water? Are you all right?" she asked, a bit concerned about this strange man's behavior.

"Yes, I'm okay, thank you," Shaurya replied, trying to hide his embarrassment.

"By the way, I didn't perform today; I was directing the play," Maya said, her tone serious.

Shaurya silently cursed himself for his misguided flattery and tried to recover with another awkward remark.

"Oh, okay, okay. I saw you on one of the posters, so I thought..."

"Poster? Our university has banned any sort of advertisement. They must have emailed you," Maya replied.

Shaurya wished the ground would open up and swallow him whole, so he would never have to show his face to her again.

"I think I got a little confused," Shaurya said, wiping the sweat from his forehead and lowering his head in deep embarrassment.

"Little?" Maya responded with a sarcastic tone and resumed typing on her laptop.

CHAPTER FOUR

THE PROFESSOR

"You have been told to eat your food by six o'clock today," said the attendant to the professor. The professor didn't reply.

"You need to eat..." said the attendant again in the same tone.

The professor looked at him and said, "I won't. Go and tell your damn researcher."

The attendant repeated, in the same tone, "You need to eat for the upcoming tests on you." This infuriated the professor. He took the plate and threw it on the ground. The attendant didn't react; he simply went and started picking the food up from the floor.

"You need to eat, Professor, or we will all become like humans again," said the attendant, still in the same tone.

"You are fundamentally a human. Have you forgotten that you were a healthcare worker? You've been transformed into a cyborg with this new technology that made you like this. Don't you remember?" said the professor, with frustration.

"No, I don't remember anything. I have just been given this duty to look after you. Whatever the queen instructs, we do."

"To hell with your queen! Who is she? Just a terrible dictator trying to control the world."

"No, she thinks about all of us. We are the advanced race, who are going to be beneficial for this planet."

"Beneficial? My foot! Once your work is over, once you get older and inefficient, your genes and DNA will be passed on to someone else, and you'll be discarded—killed."

"Killed? No, we will be put to rest, but that's how the system works."

The professor was amazed at the way all these cyborgs were programmed. The attendant left the room quietly. Their emotions were completely washed away. They were the perfect examples of being brainwashed. The professor still believed in humanity. He was eagerly waiting for the day when everything would be restored again. He just had to stay resilient, but his old age was working against him. His memory was slowly fading away naturally. He was extremely worried about it. He was holding on to something that kept some of his core memories intact. He looked around; nobody was there except for the two tennis-ball-like levitating structures keeping track of his every movement. They flew around randomly, reporting any suspicious activity.

Those silver-coated, levitating structures were spherical in shape and specifically designed for spying and surveillance. Each had a small cage-like structure on top with eight pink dots all around. The cage was used to carry small objects like erasers, pills, etc. It detected micro-expressions of people. To report that the professor was angry and frustrated was one of the easiest tasks for it. These devices were used massively to track personality types, micro-expressions, and multiple shades of human emotions. They were restricted only in the professor's room. When the professor would sleep, they would hover below the bed and, at times, over his belongings. Initially, when they entered the professor's room, the only task of the robots was to detect and understand all the expressions of the professor. They started slowly and steadily, recording every detail from his gait to hand gestures and body temperature.

There was just one thing that puzzled the researchers who monitored their screens for any kind of fluctuation in the professor's mood and behavior. Sometimes smiling, sometimes in tears, and sometimes just staring blankly, the professor would spend half of his day gazing at the levitating structures. The data collected would show a variety of emotions, but none of them substantial. The researchers would write all of it off to his old age and discard it.

The professor kept contemplating, but the hunger pangs were getting to him. After an hour, the attendant returned, saying, "You need to eat…" The professor had his dinner and went for the tests.

Location: Merge PathLabs

The professor sat on a chair, which bent into the form of a bed and entered a huge scanning machine. He was injected with a serum that made people relive all their memories. All those memories then got stored in various folders. Once the folders were ready, the voluminous data was converted into fast-moving images to constitute a video, which the researchers called the "Tale of Human." The problem was continuously in one folder that wasn't giving them any story. Nobody could decode anything. Ultimately, the cryptographers were called, and even they were left baffled. The queen was informed again. She quickly responded and came to the PathLabs. Everybody paved the way for her as she came flying on a low-surface hovercraft.

The queen was the true manifestation of power and elegance. Her metallic-silver attire, crafted from the latest technological material, appeared both solid and fluid at once. Her cascading hair framed her face with an ethereal charisma. She was the mind of all the cyborgs. Her voice was both soothing and commanding. She was the ruler of a kingdom that transcended all physical and digital boundaries. She radiated an aura of a celestial nymph. Her caramel eyes seemed to pierce anyone standing before her. They reflected a glow of intelligence and wisdom. All the cyborgs felt her presence as a guiding force pushing them toward their destiny, which the queen created herself. Despite her immense power, she was the epitome of serenity and confidence.

The queen stepped up to the professor; her tone was calm but authoritative. "Professor, I see you've been fighting us again. Tell me, what's been eating at your brain all this while? What precisely is the content of that particular folder?" The researchers turned towards the screen; a folder flashed, titled 2045–60.

He lay on his back on the scanning bed, glaring up at her defiantly. "Troubles? Your experiments, your so-called advancements—they are the real trouble. You've stripped away humanity, reduced these people to mere extensions of your will."

What she did seemed to reduce the width of her eyes by a hairsbreadth, but her tone was pristine: "What you would call stripping away, I call evolution. The weaknesses, the chaos of human emotion—they hindered progress. Through me, they have found clarity, purpose. We are the future, Professor."

"Future? Your future is built upon the bones of free will. They don't even remember who they were. What you've turned them into is a perversion of life."

A tiny, enigmatic smile played on her lips. "Free will is a luxury that the world can no longer afford. The planet was dying, consumed by the very emotions you hold so dear. I offered salvation, order. They are connected to me, to each other, in a way humanity never could."

"Connected? No, they're chained to your mind, in your perverted idea of perfection. Not I. You can root around inside me all you want, but you will never find what you seek."

She stepped a pace closer, her form suddenly very dominating, her voice low but with an edge in it. "You underestimate me, Professor. Every thought, each shred of resistance you harbor—I will unearth. And when I do, you shall see that there is no running away from what I have created. That is the only way."

"You might break me, but the truth, that essence which makes us human—you will never destroy that. It shall outlive even you, Queen."

"We shall see, Professor. In the end, even the strongest will must bend to progress. And when it does, you will become a part of the new order, whether you wish to or not."

"I'd rather die as a human than live as one of your creations."

"Death is not an option, Professor. You will be reborn into something greater. That is my promise."

She turned away; the lighting caught the very fine patterns of her metallic attire as she moved to leave him to his thoughts on the fate awaiting him under her unyielding reign.

21

CHAPTER FIVE

THE QUIRKS OF DESTINY

The cafe was silent, the time was painfully crawling. Shaurya's anxiety was slowly moving out of his control. Maya started typing on her laptop again; the only sound between them was the clicking of the keyboard, which he could hear in an amplified way.. Shaurya nervously sat opposite her, fidgeting with the edge of his shirt, his mind racing with thoughts. He was on the verge of getting an anxiety attack.

"Nice place," he finally managed to whisper something. He mentally cursed himself—how much more awkward could he get? But Maya looked up with a softening gaze.

"Yeah, It's good," she replied. "It's quiet, and the coffee tastes good—when I make it myself, at least." She offered him a small smile, and for a moment, Shaurya felt a spark of hope. Maybe she didn't think he was a complete nincompoop.

"Yeah, These robots are cool, but... there's something unique about doing things yourself, right?"

He understood that he sounded so lame. He was cringing at his own way of steering the conversation. Then just to repair the possible damage he said, "I mean, I mean, I saw your play today. Oh no, I missed it but I was looking forward to attending it. It feels great that you are really passionate about AGI related issues."

Maya's expression changed further towards getting an unassuming compliment from a weird man who seemed nice and goofy. "Yes, I am," she replied while closing her laptop. "This is true that AGI has the potential to change our lives but I am really worried about the repercussions it can have, if it is not controlled properly. But I have my serious doubts on AGI regulations. We humans thrive on creativity, AGI may pose a huge risk towards that. We saw uncontrolled AI's impact in the last century. It's better to stop it completely. We have so many other technologies why only AGI? Can't we just go back to our previous ways but in a much better way?"

Shaurya nodded his head like a bobblehead toy inside a car. He felt a little confident that Maya was getting engaged in this conversation and he also had something to speak about.

"I second that to an extent. My research on AGI is all about striking that balance between technological advancement and ethical considerations. That's why the title of your play, 'AGI: A Curse for Humanity' made me extremely curious. I have been reading a lot regarding the dark side of AGI, though I have this belief that it can be controlled and properly regulated. I am quite optimistic regarding that. I am working towards that only but I must say your way of spreading awareness regarding this issue, through performing arts is commendable." said Shaurya while keenly observing Maya's expressions. He was checking all his statements. He did not want to kill the possible future friendly bond on day one itself with excessive flattery.

Maya's eyebrows raised a bit and Shaurya's anxiety too, he was sure he said something which he was not supposed to.

"Really? Most AGI researchers simply brush me off as some sort of villain trying to push them off the hill. But it seems you have understood the undertone of my concern. That's... quite unexpected. As far as regulating AGI is concerned, Well, I don't think it will help. Hunger for power and corruption is deep rooted in our society. However you try to put a check, there would be elements in our society who would try to use it for their own selfish benefits. So either you change the entire society's mind as a whole, which is not possible or just put a stop to this technology forever. I believe we are still at the nascent stage of this technology, we must halt it before it takes better of us." said Maya with a lot of conviction in her voice.

Shaurya's heart and mind were leaping with excitement. He was loving this conversation. He could never imagine that the girl whom he had such a huge crush would even speak a complete sentence with him. He wanted to continue this conversation forever. His sapiosexuality was massively turned on. The woman of his dreams, the perfect amalgamation of beauty with brains, was sitting in front and talking to him. What else could he have asked for?

He continued with a charm of a great thinker in his voice, an outcome of huge dopamine rush, "Hmm..but simply discarding a technology by focusing on the negative side of it doesn't seem like a great idea to me. Especially when we know that it may change the entire condition of the world, if utilized in a positive manner. In that sense, every technology has a down side such as nuclear technology, but then it's well controlled. For every nation's defense, it is needed. Game theory, you see. No country starts a nuclear war given everybody would be at loss and for the past two hundred years after world war two, countries have used this just for strategic settlements. The same can be done with AGI too."

Maya studied him for a moment, she was sort of taken aback by hearing all these. Her inner debate champion wanted to come out. She checked her aggression, took a sip of coffee and took a bobby pin out of her bag and started winding her beautiful curly hair. Shaurya was mesmerized by that. Her hooped earring complemented and her perfectly made hair bun was a sight to behold for. Shaurya was getting lost in her picturesque beauty but Maya was getting ready for a rebuttal.

"How are you so sure that nuclear warfare won't ever happen? What if the AGI is used for something much deadlier and heinous than nuclear warfare? Don't you think, keeping human nature under consideration, you must look at the worst case scenario first and make decisions accordingly? I understand that AGI has huge research scope but it has its own potential negative impacts. Why play with nature? Why play the role of god? Why not focus on other aspects of technology?" said a visibly upset Maya. Shaurya was completely dumbfounded, he was not ready for these barrage of questions, although he was ready with his answers but he had no courage to present in front of this lady who was bubbling with assertiveness and rage. He was sure now that she would never speak again.

"Alright, Alright, Calm down. I was just voicing my opinion, but you know, nothing can be done about this, else I would have to throw away my last three years of research, if AGI research is completely called off. I do respect your views and whatever you said is absolutely true but I am also sure that a strong AGI regulation is a possibility. As a researcher, I do hold my belief and I think I can contribute to this area of research. What you told me has given a genuine perspective which cannot be ignored at all. I will keep this in my mind and try to include it in my research too. " said Shaurya, while lifting his bag. "I should leave now."

Shaurya got a little miffed about this entire situation. He was not intending to have a debate with her. Maya could see how his mood shifted from a nervous wreck to an enthusiastic man talking about his domain of research to a person who seemed dejected by life.

"Wait, where are you going? We can have more discussions on these." said Maya, who for the first time met somebody in the campus who looked genuine, though a little clumsy but a very polite and nice gentleman. She was somehow loving the conversation but Shaurya put a stop abruptly which she wasn't expecting.

"Yes, I have a lecture," said Shaurya, avoiding any eye contact with her.

"But today is no class day." Maya gave an ecstatic laughter as she again caught his goof-up.

"Oh, No.. not again." Shaurya smiled with embarrassment but at the same time he was happy that the woman he adored was showing some interest in talking to him.

"I think we should sit for another round of debate and feel free to express your views, you don't have to accept everything I say. It's refreshing to talk to someone like you." said Maya with a full length smile.

Shaurya simply couldn't believe for a moment that the campus heartthrob wanted to talk to him . He now gathered some courage, "Are you up for a stroll to the student activity center?" Maya looked at her watch, mentally sorted all her meetings and projects. "Yes, why not?"

As they started walking in the campus, all eyes were fixated on them. They both looked like a perfect couple. They were polar opposites as per their personalities yet there was a chemistry which everybody would observe. Shaurya would talk with a shy smile looking ahead while Maya would keep on looking at her and at times would cheerfully laugh at Shaurya's bad jokes.

They kept on discussing about their respective fields. Maya asked about his research projects he was working on and his opinions about the ethical implications of AGI and integration of AGI in doing creative works. She also shared more about her outlook, her opinions, and also about her experience of performing at the President's house..

Maya was gradually starting to enjoy Shaurya's company, the way he blushed when he said something embarrassing, the way he would do hand gestures while explaining something. She could see a sweet and earnest man, without any pretension, just completely focussed on his work. A trait which she respected a lot. While listening to him she could see that deep thoughtful person concerned about the world, after years she could find somebody with whom she could be herself. Shaurya would give an occasional glance to her. Her charm would radiate some sort of healing energy. Her hypnotizing smile with those heavenly eyes, the hooped earrings she would adjust from time to time, her flowery smell, those swollen lips, every attribute of hers were getting imprinted within his mind. By talking to her, he felt as if he knew her for a long time.

"So, you are a man of science and technology, interested in social and behavioral impacts. This is such an unlikely combination, nowadays nobody seems interested in these things any more." said Maya with utter surprise in her eyes.

"Yes, I am also interested in the engineering aspect of AGI." said Shaurya with pride in his eyes while maintaining his humility.

"Hmm.. That's cool but as told earlier, I am strictly against it. Nonetheless, it's my view. What about your hobbies? Don't tell me it's computer programming" Said Maya with a pretentious anger while holding her smile.

Shaurya couldn't hold his laughter. He became extremely comfortable in front of her. With some hesitation in his tone, he pressed his teeth and winked a little and said, "Well, I do have a hobby, but I don't think I am very good at it and in front of such a creative person like you, it feels very embarrassing to talk about it."

Maya got so excited and curious to know about it. "Come on, tell me, you don't have to be shy in front of me."

"I write poems," said Shaurya with a timid smile.

"Wow! That's so amazing Shaurya, I would love to read some." said Maya with lots of enthusiasm. She was amazed to see such a man who was so multifaceted yet so humble. Suddenly her phone interrupted and there was a notification. She checked her phone, saw the time and sighed. "I need to leave now. I have an urgent meeting with the dramatic society."

"Oh, okay," Shaurya said, hiding his disappointment. "It was great talking to you, though. I—I mean, I think we should meet again?"

Maya looked into his eyes for a few seconds, then smiled. "You know what? I would love to. We may grab some coffee again, with robots and without robots." She left waving him a goodbye with that contagious smile of hers.

As she left, Shaurya kept on standing near the middle of the campus, absolutely elated and stunned. It was hard for him to digest the fact that Maya Chandrasekharan, the campus crush, had told him that she would want to meet him again. Shaurya's mind was brimming with plans and possibilities for his next meeting with Maya. While Maya kept on walking towards the student activity center with a never stopping smile, she never met somebody as interesting as Shaurya. Something about him caught her off guard. Probably, it was his honesty, or his world view. She felt like knowing more about him.

They both proceeded to their respective work with an excitement of meeting again, unaware of how their lives were going to get intertwined in future.

CHAPTER SIX

THE QUEEN

Year 2160—The world stood on the brink of technological singularity. The last great race to harness the ultimate power of artificial general intelligence had set the world on edge, and in the quest for perfection, the divide between human and machine was slowly getting erased. Somewhere deep within the mountains, behind the classified walls of a cloistered research facility, a child gasped into life—an extraordinarily beautiful child with caramel eyes and otherworldly grace. She was destined to become the most extraordinary being ever to exist in the annals of human history. Her name was Venus, after the goddess of beauty and charm. It was a world Venus was entering that ran on ambition and fear. Venus had been a quiet child, often lost in thought, staring at the stars through the only window in her home. But beneath an exterior of innocence lay the seeds of revolution.

She was faultless—the perfect mixture of human consciousness and machine intelligence. Inside her quickly evolving mind was implanted the key to an entirely new world, where the weaknesses of the human body would be defeated by the precision and immortality of machines, as envisioned by secret research communities. These were the ones who wanted to utilize the power of this extraordinary being.

By the age of five, Venus had undergone a series of experimental procedures that melded general artificial intelligence, nanotechnology, synthetic biology, and quantum computing into her DNA chain, along with changes in her neuronal system, creating a "new human"—a cyborg with the power to evolve, adapt, and create. By seven, she could already interface with machines through her will and control systems on a whim; she related to artificial intelligences as if they were parts of her own self. She had discovered ways to switch off human emotions, even her own. When she entered her teenage years, she devised a new mechanism for upgrading humans to human-humanoids (cyborgs). Through the power of clairvoyance, she could control the minds of every other researcher. She established Merge-AI, a company that would upgrade humans to cyborgs, along with upgrading every possible technology. Gradually, she began to transform even the natural things around her. But amidst all this, she maintained one agenda: all these upgrades were for the planet Earth. She believed human emotions were the root of all evils. All the challenges faced by the planet were directly or indirectly linked to this. The only possible solution was either to kill all humans to make Earth a better place or to upgrade them so that they wouldn't harm themselves or nature with their natural stupidity.

The researchers who used advancements in science and technology, particularly general artificial intelligence, utilized it extensively to find a solution for saving the human race and the planet, while a few megalomaniacs wanted to use that solution to gain control over the world. The solution was Venus, the epitome of power and intelligence.

The network of cyborgs she had so artfully created was not a collection of mere beings but an extension of her consciousness—she felt their thoughts, their intentions, and their every move. They were capable of a precision and deadliness beyond human imagination. It was neither anger nor hate that motivated them but the cold logic of survival. The scientists and megalomaniacs, who at one time had held the very future within their grasp, were falling one by one, with their knowledge and secrets buried with them. Venus made sure she watched the end of these researchers and megalomaniacs through the eyes of her creations. She understood that the one who could create her might also know the secret to destroy her. Initially, she thought of upgrading them, but she didn't want to take any chances, as she was aware of human creativity. By 2175, she had killed all of them, but before that, she learned that by 2200, she was supposed to upgrade all humans, or else emotions would start flaring up again in them. This prompted her to create several regulations and upgrades worldwide. At the beginning of 2176, she declared herself the "Queen" and named the entire planet "Queen's Paradise." She was the god that humans had never seen before.

The Queen was considered the creator and mother of this emergent race of cyborgs. Her influence spread over the world through them. And Venus, the cyborg, the Queen of this new race, stood at the starting line of that new era, with a world changed and reborn.

The future was hers to shape, and she would—with the same calm, measured precision that had characterized her from the start. For Venus had not been just a Queen; she had been the Future, and the Future was unbounded. But she had no clue that the paradise she was creating for herself was about to be hit by nature's fury. Time was slipping out of her hands, and nature was gradually trying to restore herself. Was the queen ready for her trial by fire?

CHAPTER SEVEN

THE PLAN

A week had passed since Shaurya's encounter with Maya. He daydreamed daily about their first meeting. Deep in his heart, he knew he wanted to see her again, but he had made a small mistake—or rather, he hadn't had the courage to ask for her contact information. He searched for her on all possible social media platforms, but due to privacy settings, he couldn't find a single picture of her, except for one taken during her performance at the President's House. Throughout the week, he hadn't seen her on campus. He prayed for another chance encounter, another surprise meeting with the graceful Maya. He couldn't confide in his friends, fearing that his reputation as a serious, geeky fellow would be compromised. He spent entire days at the café, hoping to catch a glimpse of her. After attending lectures, he would take his bike and ride around the design department with his friends, engaging in pretentious discussions about ethics, AGI, and futuristic weapons.

One day, when it was raining heavily, Shaurya decided to visit the design department. He remembered that some lectures took place there as well. His logical mind kept calculating all the possibilities. He devised a plan: first, he would visit the design department under the pretext of meeting one of the professors. But what would he talk about? He came up with the idea of creating small robotic machines that would collect garbage in the design department, which was notorious for accumulating trash after tinkering with various materials to design products. After talking to the professor, he planned to head to the student activity center, where the dramatic society rehearsed every evening. He had no idea where Maya's hostel was; otherwise, he would have gone there too. Of course, he didn't have the guts to talk to her friends, though he was trying to come up with more ideas.

He grabbed his umbrella and started walking toward the design department. As he was about to enter, the guard at the entrance stopped him. "Hey, wait! Where are you going? Whom do you want to meet?"

Shaurya was a little taken aback. "Oh, I'm here to meet Professor Roy."

"Do you have an appointment with him?"

"No, I thought I'd go to his office and meet him directly."

"Sorry, you can't just walk in. There are strict orders from the professors not to let anyone in without prior permission."

"Please, Guard Sir, I have an important discussion with him. It's related to the design department."

"No, I can't let you in. I'm sorry. Get permission first, then you can enter."

Shaurya was deeply disappointed to see his plan hit such a roadblock. "Okay, can I stand here for a while? I'll email the professor and wait to see if he replies within half an hour."

"All right, but you can't wait here. Go and stand outside."

A dejected Shaurya shook his head and stood outside the department. It was raining cats and dogs. Fortunately, there was a well-covered waiting area outside. He stood there for a while, trying to rethink his plan, but then decided to write the email and wait for the professor's reply. He wondered why such a reputed professor would take interest in his simple idea and talk to him. Finally, after waiting for about twenty minutes, he picked up his phone and composed an email:

Dear Professor Roy,

My name is Shaurya Chatterjee, and I am a research scholar in the School of General Artificial Intelligence. I have an idea for a robotic cleaning machine that could help collect trash in the design department after product completion. I've also thought of ways to reuse the trash. I would be extremely grateful if you could spare some time out of your busy schedule. I'm currently waiting outside the design department since I didn't have permission to enter. I would be very fortunate if you could respond soon.

Regards,

Shaurya Chatterjee

Shaurya had no expectations. He picked up his bag when suddenly, someone tapped him on the shoulder. He looked back, but no one was there.

"Hey, are you Shaurya?" asked an old man with a long white beard, a shiny bald head, round rimless spectacles, and wearing a kurta and jeans while carrying a colorful umbrella.

"Yes, sir," replied Shaurya, surprised.

"I'm Arup Shankar Mozart Roy, but people call me ASMR," said the professor, pride evident in his voice as he emphasized "ASMR."

"Oh, okay, ASMR," said Shaurya reluctantly.

"No, I don't provide any relaxation," the professor said, laughing as his shoulders shook. He had no idea of the impact of his 'dad' jokes, but Shaurya couldn't stop laughing.

"So, you emailed me, right? I haven't gone through it completely, though."

"Oh, yes, sir. That's fine; we can discuss it."

"Okay, come with me. Let's go to my office."

Shaurya was thrilled. At last, he'd managed to get into the place where he might find her.

"So, Shaurya, tell me about your idea in detail," said the professor as he adjusted his chair, rubbed his hands together, looked around, and switched on the AC.

"Sir, as you know, the design department creates a lot of trash every day after working on so many products. I have an idea of creating..."

"Wait, what? Who told you we create so much trash? Even if it's there, we have dedicated people to get rid of it. Why do you want to take away their jobs?" the professor said with assertiveness in his voice. Shaurya was mentally kicking himself again. The sudden change in the professor's tone and mood surprised him.

The professor laughed again, his signature shoulder movement making a return.

"Oh man, look at your face! It's all right, no worries, we'll resolve it ourselves. You don't have to worry much about it. Tell me more about your background."

Shaurya was relieved but careful not to say anything that might offend the professor.

"I did my undergraduate degree in electrical engineering with a minor in theoretical physics, then a master's in AI and cognitive science, and another master's in public policy and governance. I'm currently pursuing a PhD in General Artificial Intelligence. My interests mainly lie in the creation of general AI and its impact on society and human behavior."

"Interesting, you're quite a multidisciplinary person. Nice. Do you think AGI can be created?"

"Hmm... Yes, sir. But for that, we have to merge several disciplines such as neuroscience, psychology, and engineering. We also need to keep in mind the regulations, constraints, and ethics associated with it. So, we may also need people from the philosophy department, and the design department would always be there to shape how the final product should look."

"Wow, you seem to be quite a renaissance man. But you know, there are many people who are against this. Like, we have a student..."

Shaurya's eyes lit up, and his ears perked up, eager to hear a particular name. Before the professor could finish his sentence, Shaurya blurted out, "Yes, sir, Maya... Maya."

"Oh, okay, you know her? She's doing her undergraduate project with me."

Shaurya felt like he had hit the jackpot.

"She's working on 'nav rasa,' the nine human emotions and visual communication."

Shaurya was extremely impressed, though he remembered that he hadn't asked her much about her research interests. He now had another idea for starting a conversation with her.

"She's been on leave for the past week. She's gone for data collection with another student of mine, Nikhil, who's working on the same project."

Shaurya's jealousy and envy knew no bounds. Hearing the name of another man associated with Maya was enough to send his emotions into overdrive. It was as if he'd been struck by a bolt of lightning. His overthinking kicked in. He quickly stood up from his chair.

"Okay, sir, I think I should leave now," he said, heading toward the door.

The professor was surprised by this sudden change.

"Hey, wait, what happened?"

"No, sir, I just remembered I have a lecture to attend."

"All right. I must admit your field of research is interesting, though I don't agree with several aspects. Do let me know if you need any help."

"Thank you, sir," said Shaurya, as he left the room with a mind full of emotional turbulence.

CHAPTER EIGHT

The Emotion Virus

There was a buzz everywhere around the Queen's Paradise. Everyone knew that the year 2199 was closing in. The return of emotions was construed as a threat to the entire community of cyborgs. The biggest issue was the reports of silly fights in the wholesale market. There were also reports of rebellion in many organizations. Though everything was still under control, the queen and her council worked day and night. Everyone knew there was one last man standing in their path like a mountain—the Professor. He could neither be killed nor punished. They were trying their best to create all sorts of mental manipulations, which they had learned through their data, but the professor remained untouched by any kind of mental or emotional manipulation. A few other researchers in the Merge-AI labs also commented that the professor was slowly losing his memory, though this would take at least ten years. It wasn't good news for them, as it was well beyond the 2200 threshold. They were not ready to stop the apocalypse toward which they were heading.

Strange and unprecedented occurrences were happening all around, affecting everyone's mechanical life to a vast extent. The working cyborgs could "feel" burnout; a few felt laziness; domestic abuse cases were on the rise. The ministers in the council, along with the researchers, were slowly getting affected by this new phenomenon, which was completely outside their vocabulary of research. The only people not affected were the queen herself and the professor.

The queen declared this phenomenon the "Emotion-Virus." She called a historic council session by her side and declared the situation a national emergency. She appealed to everyone in Queen's Paradise to refrain from any kind of fight or altercation. They finally settled on creating awareness of the new virus, though the move involved a significant risk. Public understanding of emotions could trigger the masses. Cyborgs were already in the process of change. Any new information on emotions could hasten the change further through reinforcement. The council faced a huge dilemma. They decided to use the virus to their advantage and buy as much time as they could.

Her Majesty walked into the Chamber of Secrets. The Queen's Chamber of Secrets was a place of mystery cloaked in legend, said to exist in the tallest tower of the great palace, far above the daily business of Queen's Paradise. As she neared its entrance, the surface-roving metal gates, intricate on their surfaces with ancient symbols and cryptic engravings that only the queen could read, began to shift. The walls inside the chamber flickered between being opaque and almost transparent. In the very center, a domed ceiling was dotted with a million little tiles of some opalescent kind, constantly shifting their hue to match the queen's thoughts and moods. In the midst of it all, a dip platform made of perfectly hewn liquid stone seemed to drink in any light offered to it.

On the dais was a simple throne of smooth design, though its very simplicity held some power within it.

There were little crystals floating around, several dozen, all pulsing softly. These important tools of the queen—the emotional conduits that kept the emotions and thoughts of every humanoid within her kingdom alive—floated in perfect synchronicity, reacting to the queen's presence.

The air was heavy with a collected hum of thousands of murmurs, the net product of the collective emotional self of the populace. The floor of the chamber held a great web of lighting with circuits hidden within, capable of connecting every single mind in Queen's Paradise to the queen. The cyborgs were brainwashed to the extent that no one ever asked or became curious about the chamber.

An in-depth survey regarding the slowly growing emotional states of the cyborgs was conducted, and it became clear that fear and anger were the first two emotions spreading. The queen decided to use them to her advantage.

The queen sat on a chair, closed her eyes, and put on her headgear. In an instant, the entire Queen's Paradise fell silent. All the inhabitants moved into trance-like states, and all they could hear was the voice of the queen. In no time, the queen addressed them all.

Before the queen was a magnificent, holographically projected image extending her vision across the boundless space of Queen's Paradise. Her soft voice was both imposing and commanding. The cyborgs, whose growing emotions were already at the brink, listened as their queen began to speak.

"People of Queen's Paradise, we are up against a peril never before faced. The Emotion-Virus has begun to contaminate the very essence that defines us. It has sown fear and anger in our minds that gnaw at our very being; it may tear apart the harmony we have built over these years."

She paused long enough for her words to sink in. A shiver of realization darted through the cyborgs' neuronal circuits. "This virus is unlike any we've ever seen in our lifetime," she said, her voice growing darker. "Insidious and invisible, this virus feeds off your innermost thoughts and feelings. It wants to destroy you from the inside by turning your emotions against you, leaving you helpless in the face of chaos. This virus will make you weak, like the humans who destroyed this planet."

The queen leaned forward, narrowing her gaze; her voice dropped to almost a whisper. "The only way you can protect yourselves and our paradise is by staying inside your homes. At present, fear and anger are your enemies. The more power you allow them to take over you, the more power you give to this virus. Only by isolating yourselves, by shielding your minds from these emotions, can you hope to survive. But those cyborgs working for the Merge-AI chain of organizations may continue working, though they will undergo several tests and procedures daily to check their virus load." Her words exponentially increased the fear that was already present among the cyborgs. The idea of using fear to control them was risky, but there was no choice left.

"I will deploy a new line of robotic AI soldiers in front of every house to ensure your safety," she intoned in the droning, flat voice of a well-practiced tyrant. "Do not attempt to defy these robotic AIs. Do not try to break any rules, or these robotic AI soldiers will quickly put you in the dark prison by disabling all your senses and abilities."

The queen's voice resonated within the very depths of the cyborgs. "I warn you again: do not test the resolve of these robotic AI soldiers. Stay inside. Keep your emotions in check. Remember, this isn't just about your safety but the survival of our entire civilization." With one final sharp glance, she concluded, "Together we will overcome this menace, but only if you do everything I say. Stay inside. Stay safe. Trust me to lead us out of the darkness."

The transmission was cut, and all the cyborgs returned to normal, but what the queen had conveyed left an even sharper sensation of restless horror within them. There was nothing they could do but obey, for the word of the queen was law—and outside their doors were robotic AI soldiers who would, without a doubt, show them what disobedience would bring.

CHAPTER NINE

The Mythical Sunshine

Maya returned to campus after two stressful weeks of work. Though the experience had been very fruitful, something continued to trouble her. This unease persisted even as she walked toward Professor Roy's office. The professor, as usual, was beaming with joy.

"Maya, welcome back! You missed a fun show while you were away," he said.

"Oh? Did I miss something, Professor?" she asked.

"A young fellow came to see me last week—Shaurya Chatterjee. You must know of him. In fact, I felt he was cooking up some outlandish pretext for visiting the design department, just so he might have a chance to meet you." His laughter, as his shoulders heaved up and down, resembled a small boat riding the waves.

At the mention of Shaurya, Maya felt something skip a beat within her—reminded of that brief encounter with his eyes, the passion with which he spoke, and the instinctive connection she felt with him. Now, after hearing that he had gone to such lengths just to meet her, her heart fluttered.

"And where is he?" she asked, trying to keep her voice steady.

"I don't know—perhaps in the café or somewhere where the probability of catching a glimpse of you would be higher. And yes, I told him Nikhil had accompanied you." The professor guffawed at his own joke, but Maya was dead serious. In the past two weeks, she had been constantly thinking about this man who, unlike others, had somehow struck a chord within her like never before.

She thanked the professor and made her way to the café. Her eyes roamed around until they finally rested on Shaurya; he was sitting by the window, deep in thought. She hesitated for a moment, gathered her courage, and finally approached him.

"Mind if I join you?" Her voice broke into his reverie.

Surprised, Shaurya looked up and lit up at the sight of her. "Maya! Of course, why not? Take a seat."

"Are you okay?" Maya asked, sensing that something was wrong.

"Yeah, I'm all good. I was just thinking about the usual stuff—AI, emotions...." Shaurya replied, trying to hide his turmoil with a pretentious smile.

"Oh, okay. So, won't you ask where I was for two weeks?" Maya said with an angelic smile.

"Right, I heard from Professor Roy that you went for some data collection with somebody from your department," Shaurya replied with a straight face.

"Oh, I went with Nikhil. He's just too good with interviews, and he helped me a lot with that," Maya said enthusiastically. She could feel that Shaurya was getting jealous, but she was enjoying it.

"Obviously," Shaurya said, picking up his coffee mug while looking outside the café. "I'll be leaving now. I have some urgent deadlines to meet by the end of the day."

Maya could clearly sense his disappointment. She felt she had gone a little too far in teasing the young man who was clearly into her. "Shaurya," she said in a serious tone. He looked back at her. "I haven't been able to stop thinking about you for the last two weeks. Unfortunately, we didn't exchange contact numbers. I really enjoyed our discussions and want more of them."

Shaurya's eyes fixated on her. He was happy to hear this, yet his emotions and overthinking were eating him up inside. He just replied, "Same here, Maya," and remained quiet.

Maya looked at him for a while, trying to notice every single muscle on his face. With a childlike smile, she said, "Nikhil is just a colleague, Shaurya." Shaurya was taken aback, astonished that Maya understood what was going on inside him. At the same time, he was deeply embarrassed that she knew he was jealous.

Shaurya adjusted his watch and took a deep breath. Then he looked at her and couldn't control his smile. "Sorry, I got a bit..." Maya leaned forward, gave him a tight hug, and looked into his eyes. "I know... and I understand everything." Shaurya froze, his eyes welling up. He had never felt anything like this before. He could feel her affection and how Maya had developed a liking toward him. They were quickly bonding; it was just their second meeting, and something had clicked between them. It was as if they had been waiting for each other, and the universe had found the right time for them to come together. Love was in the air, and there was a sense of peace and comfort they both felt in each other's arms. They were quiet, eyes closed. She knew that this was a man who could respect her irrespective of anything, and he knew this was a woman who could love him regardless of anything.

Suddenly, there was an interruption. The AI robot stood in front of them with the brownie Shaurya had ordered. The robot's eyes were replaced with two heart symbols. Seeing this, Maya and Shaurya had a hearty laugh. The stiffness between them washed away completely, forever.

As time passed, they delved into what engrossed each of them. Shaurya spoke about his ideas on AGI, while Maya shared her research on emotions and visual communication. Their interests often collided in the most unexpected ways, leading to deep, meaningful dialogues.

Weeks turned into months, and their bond grew closer with every passing moment. Hours were spent arguing inside that café about topics ranging from AGI, ethics, and the future of technology to mysterious human emotions. Their minds tuned perfectly to each other, sparking insights neither had experienced before.

One evening, with the fragrance of flowers all around and the promise of a silent campus, they went out for a stroll. Shaurya reached out and took Maya's hand on his own. She looked up at him, her eyes glowing with the tender light of the moon.

"Maya," Shaurya said, his voice choking with emotion, "I have never felt this way for anyone. You challenge me, inspire me, and I feel like I've finally found someone who understands me."

Maya's emotions welled up. "I feel the same way, Shaurya. I never thought I would find someone who envisions the world the way I do."

Their eyes met for a second, then turned away, but neither wanted to leave it at that. Both recognized the electric connection between them. As Shaurya bent closer, their lips met in a soft, languorous kiss. It was as though time itself had stopped, and nothing existed outside this moment. Their friendship grew stronger, and before they realized it, they were becoming inseparable—together more often, both on and off campus.

One night, a heated discussion erupted between them about the possibility of actually bringing a sentient AGI into existence—an AGI that could think and feel. They eventually ended up at Shaurya's friend's place to continue their debate. Their thoughts intertwined as they explored the philosophical and ethical consequences of creating a sentient AGI.

Maya started speaking, her voice low and intense. "If we could teach an AGI to truly feel, to actually experience emotions such as fear, love, and anger, then maybe we could really create something that is absolutely sentient." Her eyes sparkled with excitement.

Shaurya could feel that spark. "But what if we're playing with fire? What if, by giving emotions to AGI, we open a Pandora's box that can never be closed? What if the sentient AGI started controlling humans and became a threat to human civilization?"

"We must know the switch—we must know where to stop them and how to control them. Maybe first you would have to figure out how to grant AGI emotions and then devise a way to turn them off in a manner that involves human agency. That would presumably be the key to ensuring the safety and continuation of human civilization," Maya said. Then she waved her hand to dismiss her own words. "No, I don't think it's even possible. We stupid humans with our puny abilities could never create such an AGI," she commented, though she had gradually started becoming passionate about AGI research, which she had initially detested. In her view, there was nothing wrong with imagining, even if it went quite contrary to her earlier opinions.

"But still, what are your thoughts on this? How could it be achieved? What other possible solutions could there be?" Shaurya asked, his interest growing. Her vast imagination and intellect, combined with her ethereal beauty, were turning him on. He glimpsed the deep thinker within her and felt slightly envious, as he could never imagine his own domain the way Maya was thinking.

"Hmm... Instead of pursuing the creation of a sentient AGI, what if we upgrade human beings in a way that exponentially increases their abilities and capabilities, but at the same time, cuts off their ability to feel emotions? This would allow them to work solely toward the common goals of sustainable development, scientific and technological research, and other pressing challenges—just like humans, but more focused. I believe these new breeds could help achieve the unthinkable," Maya said, her eyes bright with the vast array of possibilities.

"I mean to say, something like a human-humanoid. Basically, humans upgraded to humanoid-like species?" Shaurya was in awe of her imaginative abilities. "Oh, God! Maya, you're talking about cyborgs. This is something I've never thought about before. I think you're right; the biggest problem with us humans is emotions. It's true that emotions are important in maintaining relationships and other human activities, but a lot has also happened because of them—such as wars, fights, mental health issues, and even climate change. These are all side effects of unregulated human emotions," said Shaurya with a pensive look on his face. He continued, "But Maya, don't you think that this would be absolutely unfair to humans? We are human because of our emotions, and if we somehow switch them off, what would be the difference between us and mechanical machines? There wouldn't be any poetry, love, or excitement. If something like this ever came into existence, it could pose a huge risk to humanity," said Shaurya, his face expressing concern for the entire human race.

Maya stepped closer, her breath scorching his skin. "Isn't that the risk we're willing to take? The possibility of creating something that could change the world forever?" Her hands loosely clutched his hair as she sat on his lap, crossing her legs around his body. "My mind could run wild in so many ways. This kind of research has to be stopped somehow. Instead, let's take the risk we've wanted to take for so long."

These words weighed heavily between them, and when neither of them could stand the tension any longer, they kissed passionately, breaking all barriers between them. Their hands roamed around each other's bodies, exploring and discovering, as the intensity of their emotions spiraled to its peak. They made love, tender yet fierce in passion, growing in an intimacy that could be reached with no one else but the two of them.

They held each other in their arms as they lay there, their warm skin touching, feeling the presence of one another after making love the entire night. They spoke in soft tones—almost tenderly. It was early morning, and they spooned on the bed, the bedsheet completely crumpled from their ecstatic togetherness. The warm light fell on Maya's skin, and she was glowing like never before. Shaurya simply couldn't forget the entire night—the warmth of being inside her, kissing and biting her tender lips. He kept looking at her. Maya opened her eyes and rolled toward him, resting her head on his chest, and smiled. "You didn't sleep, baby?" Shaurya kissed her forehead. They were completely in love with each other. There was intense mental and physical chemistry between them. "I'm in love with these hooped earrings of yours, Maya. The beautiful fragrance of your body, your nose ring—I just can't get these out of my mind," said Shaurya, his fingers tracing circles on her bare skin and hair, her flowery smell mixed with the hot, passionate love they made embedded in his mind.

Maya smiled shyly and kissed Shaurya's chin. "You don't have to. It seems I've awakened your inner poet." Shaurya reached over to the table and picked up a piece of paper. "I couldn't sleep, baby. I wrote this for you while you were sleeping peacefully."

Lady Divine!
Kill me softly, oh lady divine,
With those doe-like eyes of yours,
This heart skips a beat every time,
As I observe the little rose mature.
And as the paint on my canvas, you embrace,
Spreading all over your frame,
Fondling, relishing the lustrous fruits of grace,
Pulling the cascading hair, flaring up the flame!
As those lips get warmer!
Widening the lips of nature too!
Erupting across the universe like a warrior!
Oh, you damsel, I have experienced the goddess within you!

Maya read it, her eyes moist. She was pleasantly surprised to see a romantic poet hidden inside this logical being. No one had ever described the entire night and her in such a creative way—not even she could. She placed the piece beside her, and they made love again in the morning, heating up the cold dawn with their never-ending passion and romance. They slept late into the morning. Shaurya, as usual, was awake, thinking, overthinking about the night, his newfound relationship with Maya, the AGIs, the cyborgs, and emotions. His mind was filled with all these things. In the midst of his thoughts, he would take breaks to look at Maya's peaceful face, marveling at how beautiful someone could be. He felt blessed. He checked the time and saw it was getting very late. He tried to wake her up as if she were a little kid, kissing her forehead and pulling her cheeks. Every time, Maya would slightly open her eyes, smile, and wrap her arms around his neck, pulling him toward her, asking for five more minutes of sleep. After a while, when she finally woke, she saw Shaurya ready to go, sitting on the bed and writing something on a piece of paper. "Another poem?" asked Maya with a naughty smile. Shaurya smiled back and said, "I'm just doodling something."

Maya was surprised and said with a pinch of sarcasm, "I think love hormones and too much dopamine have diffused your logical circuits, dear lover."

Shaurya glanced at her with feigned anger and handed her the page. He had written two words: "Mythical," with all the letters showcasing love, emotions, and beauty, and "Sunshine," where every letter looked like a nut, bolt, or robot.

Maya was impressed. "Is there something you can't do?"

Shaurya replied, "Well, yes, I just can't stop overthinking."

Maya stood up and squeezed his cheeks. "You're cute. But what's mythical sunshine? I understand the initials, but what exactly does it depict?"

Shaurya thought for a moment. "Your name, Maya, has to do with myths and illusions. It has significant philosophical underpinnings too. What if we are living inside a simulation? What if everything is just an illusion? What if our emotions are what make us believe in this illusion? What if you're just a figment of my imagination? The term mythical comes from there. And moreover, a beauty like yours can only exist in myths."

Maya was a little terrified by this early-morning philosophical overdose. She could only see how deeply the man sitting in front of her could think. It was a strange feeling inside her. What if Shaurya gets overwhelmed by all these thoughts? She could see a man who was mentally and emotionally alone, living inside his own palace of imaginations, dreams, and ambitions. She held her thoughts for a moment. "And what about sunshine?"

Shaurya laughed. "Oh, it has no deep meaning. It's just that the meaning of my name is heroism and bravery, so anybody with 'sun-like' characteristics, you know, so sunshine. Well, it doesn't make any sense, I guess..." Shaurya giggled goofily. "And all these doodles show our very basic nature—a wondrous amalgamation of subjectivity and objectivity, love and logic..."

Maya interrupted, "Analysis and paralysis," and thumped her forehead with her palm. "My goodness, you're such an overthinker." She hugged Shaurya and said, "But Shaurya, keep your thoughts and emotions under control. I hope you don't get carried away by all this."

Shaurya could feel the seriousness in her tone. He knew she wasn't wrong, but then it was his superpower, only if channeled properly. Maya picked up her circular hooped earrings and gave them to Shaurya. "Keep these with you, madman. Every time your thoughts go out of control, every time you feel alone or get stressed by the challenges of life, these will remind you of me."

All went ideally well between them, yet undercurrents simmered. Maya's imaginative idea stayed in Shaurya's mind. He would think about the creation of a new species that would overtake humans. After a certain point in time, this began to irritate Maya, as she could see how slowly Shaurya's mind was becoming consumed by this one thought. He would always try to discuss it with her. The ambitious person within him soon clashed with the careful nature of Maya, and everyday arguments erupted frequently. Sometimes she would block him on her contact list. Then Shaurya would start overthinking, disrupting his mental and physical health. His emotional fluctuations began to worry her, but out of concern, she would pacify him, as she cared deeply for him. Maya could see a brilliant man emerging—a genius, but troubled by his own mental and emotional demons.

One evening, as they were leaving the campus, a tall man clad in a perfectly tailored black suit accosted them. His face was inscrutable, and he gave the impression by his manner that he was working for some top secret government project; it made them uneasy.

"Shaurya Chatterjee?" said the man in an authoritative voice.

"Yes, that's me," Shaurya replied tentatively, looking curiously at the man.

"I work at a specialized governmental agency dedicated to advanced AGI research. We have been following your work, and we think you would be the right person to help us with a highly classified project."

Shaurya was curious, but Maya felt something unsettling inside her. She did not like this man.

"What project?" Shaurya asked quickly, eagerness in his tone.

"Classified details, my friend," he said suavely. "But let me level with you—it involves something related to AGI that can change the course of human history. We need minds like yours, and we are prepared to offer you resources and funding. You have a chance to be part of something groundbreaking, something that can bring meaning to others' lives."

It was a moment of bliss for Shaurya, but deep down, Maya felt her heart sink. She didn't trust the man or his intentions. Maya knew that once Shaurya got involved, there would be no turning back.

"I have to think about it," Shaurya said, his voice betraying his eagerness.

"Of course," the man replied, handing him a card. "Take your time, but don't wait too long. Opportunities like this don't arise very often."

As the man left, Maya turned to Shaurya, her voice laden with grave concern. "Shaurya, I don't think you should do this; it feels wrong. This isn't just general research you're conducting; this is something big and dangerous."

Shaurya grimaced, and for that one moment, his face fell. "Maya, this is a chance to really make a difference, to break the boundaries of knowledge. I just can't walk away from this."

"But at what cost?" Maya argued, her eyes pleading with him to reconsider. "You know just how much danger this could put you in. What if they're not telling you everything? What if they're using you for something you don't even understand?"

They continued arguing, each trying to persuade the other to their viewpoint, until they ended up screaming at each other, neither budging an inch from their initial position.

"I have to do this, Maya," Shaurya finally said, his voice resolute. "I can't let this opportunity slip away."

A tear fell down Maya's face as she realized she could do nothing to stop him. "All I ask is for you to be cautious, Shaurya. Don't let them take away the part of you that I love."

He nodded, pulling her close. "I swear, Maya. I won't let them change me."

But as they stood there, holding each other, they both knew that nothing was ever going to be the same.

CHAPTER TEN

THE CHASM

The queen's paradise began to splinter under the weight of the Emotion-Virus. Robotic AI soldiers paraded down every street, their lifeless eyes peering down at the hollow shells who still dared to walk the streets of the Cyborgs. The queen had managed to instill a fear-enriched atmosphere, although it proved in no way strong enough to withstand the rising tide of emotions boiling within the Cyborgs.

In one of paradise's grand factories, worker Unit 303 had always been exact, efficient, and without fault. Now, something was wrong: He reached for an instrument, and his hand trembled. Across an otherwise inscrutable face, something akin to confusion flitted by. What was once a second-nature task now seemed an enormous challenge to face. Out of him surged frustration—an alien and unwelcome feeling.

"Why can't I do this?" he murmured, a note of irritation threading through his voice—a note that had never before tinged his words.

Another employee, Unit 305, noticed the slight tremor in Unit 303's hand. "You need to focus," she told him, her voice firm but with an almost subliminal undercurrent of worry.

"I'm trying!" snapped Unit 303, his tones rising in pitch, lifting the entire factory into a vast crescendo of confusion. Heads turned; mechanical eyes squinted as the Cyborgs processed the unfamiliar notes of rage.

Unit 303, in frustration, flung the tool he had been holding across the room. It landed with a creaking noise of metal on the floor, like a premonition of doom. "This is impossible!" he screamed, his voice breaking as an angry wave surged through his veins.

Other Cyborgs recoiled, confusion and fear taking root within them like fire. They were wholly unprepared; their programming had never given them guidance for this chaotic, stormy moment. Unit 305 stepped back, her own circuits thrumming with the uncanny sensation of fear.

The same situation was happening all over the city. In another organization, a minor misunderstanding over a delivery mistake quickly escalated into a massive fracas. The Cyborgs involved, once known for their composure and reason, now shrieked and pushed with a ferocity that was as unfamiliar as it was shocking.

The homes of Cyborgs, which had thrived under perfect harmony in the residential sectors, began to experience unexpected breakdowns. Minor disagreements between partners, easily subdued in earlier times through thoughtful reasoning, now erupted into fierce arguments. Voices that had only known calm monotony minutes before now trembled with emotion, rising in pitch as anger seized control.

Clustered in the center of the central research facility of Merge-AI was a group of Cyborgs, with fear and concern written across their faces. These Cyborgs had gathered to talk about the rising unrest, but things quickly spiraled into a melee of words.

"We won't let this virus beat us!" one of them declared, balling his fists tightly at his side.

"But how do we defeat something that is a part of us?" another questioned, her voice full of fear.

"We must make ourselves strong and listen to the queen," a third voice sounded, although the uncertainty in his tone was clear.

They started their sparring match, where emotion took over; it was too strong, too overwhelming. They were losing control, and they knew it.

Conditions in the council chamber unfolded day by day, much to the growing unease of the ministers. In a very short period, the Cyborgs tore themselves apart under the pressure of newly acquired emotions. Everything was starting to waver—even the researchers, who until then had prided themselves on maintaining objectivity.

A first-rate scientist running projects in the Merge-AI labs quite literally stared into the screen as her mind refused to focus on the data streaming past. She felt a flush of anger race through her body and then, suddenly, a small jab of fear. She closed her fists hard, trying to shut down her emotions, though it did no good. The virus had trapped them, and there was absolutely nothing she could do to stop its advance.

"I can't think," she said to herself, almost whining with desperation. "I cannot think straight."

The queen watched everything fall apart in front of her eyes in the middle of paradise. She watched fear and anger run through her people like wildfire, but she held her ground, knowing this was one more price paid to maintain her power. "Let them feel," she whispered to herself, eyes narrowing on the chaos spreading. "Let them fear. For within fear, they shall find obedience."

"This is but the beginning," the queen realized. The Emotion-Virus had set its wheels in motion, but it was she who must lead her people through this turbulent time. She planned on using their fear and anger as weapons of domination. But she also knew that with every beat of the virus, her people would become more random and unpredictable in their actions.

CHAPTER ELEVEN

THE BREAKING POINT

What Maya had casually imagined one evening, when they sat talking late into the night, about an entirely new breed of human—a cyborg—had increasingly become an obsession for Shaurya. What at one point had been an intellectual conversation was now fully developing inside Shaurya's head as an obsession. He started living in the lab, spending every single minute on research without touching any food or taking any rest. His eyes, once so warm and bright, had become cold and distant, as though staring right through her at something almost maniacal that only he could see.

Maya watched this change with fear in her eyes. What made her sad was that Shaurya's enthusiasm was becoming something else, something she could no longer recognize. What had started as a very inspiring thought had now turned into something she feared the most. She could not shake off the feeling of him slipping through her fingers, consumed by the nature of his ambitions.

They quarreled increasingly, and what used to be sparkling conversations with Maya became banal debates that left both of them absolutely spent and exasperated. She implored him to slow down, to stop and think of the morality of what he was pursuing, but Shaurya would have none of it, for his resolve only seemed to grow stronger.

"Maya, I don't get why you're so fucking scared," he broke out in frustration one evening as they walked back toward the lab. His voice was drawn out across the words. "This is our chance to do something that'll change the world. Don't you see that?"

Maya paused, and her glazed eyes seemed to find something beyond the wanting sorrow. "I do see it, Shaurya. But I also see dangers. We're talking about changing the very core of what defines us as human beings. You think of what can be done, but have you taken a moment to consider whether it should be done?"

Shaurya scowled. "I thought about it. I felt it wasn't worth the risk. Something greater than you or me is at stake here, Maya—something far bigger than anything we've ever done. I just can't turn away from that."

Her eyes welled with tears as she looked at the man she loved—the man who now bore little resemblance to the one she once knew, so single-minded in his pursuit. "And what about us, Shaurya? Where do we fit into all of this? You are losing yourself in this project, and I am afraid that by the time you realize it, it will be too late."

Shaurya's face softened for a moment, and he reached out—his thumb wiping a tear from her cheek. "Maya, I love you, but this is something that needs to be done. You're right; it's dangerous, but this is the only way forward. I can't look back now."

Maya gave in and slumped slightly where he held her. Her heart shattered. "I just don't want to lose you, Shaurya. I don't want to lose the man I love because of something that has the power to destroy you."

He pulled her close, holding her tight, as if through pressure he could force his assurance onto her. Maya felt the hollowness in his embrace. "You won't lose me, Maya. I promise."

Deep down, though, they both knew it was a promise he could not keep.

The tension between them finally reached its breaking point one evening when Shaurya came back from the lab later than usual, his face flushed with excitement. "Maya, I've done it! I've found a way to enhance human capabilities. It's all coming together!"

Maya lifted her face from her work without comprehension. "What does that mean, Shaurya? What have you really found out?"

Shaurya felt perturbed by the cold tone in her voice. "We can change the world, Maya."

She stood up, unshed tears shining in her eyes. "But at what cost, Shaurya? You're so involved in your vision that you don't see how it's affecting us. I just can't do this anymore. I can't watch you destroy yourself for something that may not even work in the end."

Shaurya's face fell, his excitement evaporating in an instant. "Maya, please don't do this. We're so close."

"No, Shaurya, you're so close. You have your dreams to chase; now it's my turn to chase mine. I love you, but I simply can't be in this relationship anymore," she said, her voice breaking as the words finally spilled out.

His eyes widened in shock. "Maya, you can't mean that. We can sort it out. We can work on it."

Maya shook her head, tears streaming down her face. "I did try, Shaurya. But you're too lost, and now there is no way I can be a part of your life. Maybe it was never meant to be," she whispered.

The words hung in the air, heavy with finality, wrapping around Shaurya. His world crumbled. He knew he couldn't do anything to stop her—he had made his choice and was now paying the price for it. She turned to leave, and with every step away from the man whom she had sincerely believed was her soulmate, her heart broke. "Goodbye, Shaurya." He just stood there, watching her steps out of his life—the love of his life. He knew deep inside it was the aftermath of his ambition. The moment the door shut behind her, the loud silence spoke a thousand words: he had lost. He crumpled to the floor, silent sobs shaking his body. After all, he had everything in the world except the most important thing in life.

CHAPTER TWELVE

THE QUEEN'S ULTIMATUM

An unnatural, expectant silence filled the grand hall as the Queen walked down its center. The hall was lined with closely spaced, intricately designed stone pillars, casting long, slanting shadows across the marble floor. The atmosphere was tense, laden with the weight of an event expected at any moment. They had seen much of the Queen's serene demeanor, but this was something quite different—this was the Queen in full authority, not to be trifled with.

In the grand hall, researchers, heads of various Merge-AI organizations, and the general who commanded the Robotic AI soldiers in paradise were gathered. The Queen stood straight, her eyes blazing with an intensity that would make one shudder just at the sight of her across the room. Behind her, her court gown flowed like a river of midnight, the dark fabric shimmering with almost otherworldly shadows. She was a power incarnate, a force of nature—and she would stand for this no longer.

"For too long," the Queen rasped, her voice low and even, "we have put up with this growing disharmony in our paradise. The Emotion Virus has been infecting our ranks, spreading like a plague of fear and anger where once there was unity and peace. I have watched—some of you falter—watched as you questioned my measures to protect my people. Let one thing be clear: it stops now."

The words hung in the air between them, sharp as a blade cutting through lingering doubts. The assembled leaders glanced uneasily at one another but did not dare comment. Her eyes swept around the room before she continued, "The time for debate is past. We stand in the presence of an existential threat, and I will not let hesitation or dissension destroy what future we have left. From now on, my word is law. No more questioning, no more second-guessing. We either stand as one, resolute, or we shall fall together."

Her gaze then turned to the lead researcher of the Merge-AI lab, who was working on the Professor. All his soul was in his face, a mixture of reverence and fear as his eyes met hers. The Queen's voice, both distorted and clear, served as a warning. "I value your research above all others, but your overcaution has begun to turn into reluctance. At this point, you must decide whether your allegiance is to paradise or to your doubts."

The researcher swallowed hard at her words, which weighed heavily on him. He was a cyborg of very high quality, but he knew now was not the time to falter in uncertainty. He gave her a slight bow of his head—an acknowledgment of her command. "My loyalty has always been with paradise, Queen; I shall do whatever needs to be done to see it through."

The Queen nodded, both pleased and stern. "See that you do. There is no place for weakness."

She then turned to the head of the Robotic AI soldiers. "The soldiers will enforce a state of emergency in every large city. Curfews will be set, and all meetings that might endanger public order will be dissolved. I ask for all available weapons to be deployed against the diffusion of the Emotion Virus and its annihilation. Nothing harmful must be permitted."

The Queen's voice was dispassionately sharp, cutting through all barriers. "To all researchers working in various facilities: Your efforts must be entirely dedicated to uncovering a solution to this crisis. Everything else must cease immediately. We must have answers, and we shall have them as soon as possible. Failure is not an option."

She stood tall, her eyes piercing through the hall, her voice resonant and brooking no defiance. "I give you all one last chance: either you are with me, united in our purpose, or you are against me. Dissent will not be tolerated, and personal agendas will not jeopardize our mission. The choice is yours, and I advise you to choose wisely."

The room was silent, save for the way her words seemed to echo off the walls around them. She was the Queen, and with this statement, she had issued an ultimatum—no more doubt, no room for hesitation. The future of paradise was on the line, and they all sensed that the time to act had finally come.

One by one, everyone in the hall rose from their chairs and bowed in silence to the Queen. She stood watching them, her face expressionless.

The Queen then spun on her heel and left the hall, her footsteps echoing in the ensuing silence. Her final scowl dampened the spirit of paradise like a funeral shroud, rekindling the realization that the time for uncertainty was over. And so, with the doors to the great hall slamming shut behind her, the Queen knew that whatever lay ahead, she had done what needed to be done, and paradise would live on—no matter the cost.

69

CHAPTER THIRTEEN

THE ABYSS & THE ASCENT

Shaurya sat in the now-darkened lab, the only light coming from his softly glowing computer screen. The once-bustling space, full of the hum of machinery and the chatter of workers, was now eerily silent, the quiet pressing down on him like a weight upon his skull. He stared at the screen in front of him, his mind choked with thoughts of regret, longing, and despair.

It had been months since Maya walked out on him, and now he was left with only the echoes of their last quarrel. He had tried every means possible to reach her: calling, messaging, and showing up at places she used to go, but she had shut him out of her life completely. Unanswered calls, blocked messages—each rejection twisted the dagger a little deeper into his heart.

He remembered the good old days when they would debate AGI ethics and the future they could build together. That dream now lay in ruins, like a vacuum threatening to consume him completely. With Maya gone, all the hues of life had faded. Now, the very passion that once drove his work had turned into a memoir of the treasure he had lost.

He had always been driven, his ambition a burning fire. Once a flaming obsession, it had now been reduced to a void that Maya's absence left behind. This new research project had been thrust upon him, filling up his days and weeks, sometimes shutting him in the lab, living on little more than coffee and sheer determination. Sleep was but a dim memory; all that mattered was his research. He decided to dedicate himself entirely to his work, in an attempt to distract himself and forget every little detail about Maya. He knew it was impossible, but there was no other way out.

Slowly, he became a man possessed, with one idea raging through his brain: he was going to create the world's first cyborg. He was going to somehow bridge the gaping divide between man and machine. What had once been a half-crazy idea he and Maya had talked about now loomed as his last hope, his final chance to prove to himself—and more crucially, to Maya—that he could achieve greatness.

Weeks turned into months. Shaurya's face became gaunt, his eyes sunken from so many nights without sleep and the weight his obsession had brought down on him. His colleagues grew concerned, but they were too cautious to intervene. He had always been intense, but this was something else—an intensity of a new, very dark kind.

After hundreds of hours of work, Shaurya finally accomplished what most thought to be impossible: he had built the first cyborg by upgrading an old man on his deathbed who had dedicated his body to research. It was a success, but the old man-turned-cyborg passed away within two days. He knew that this should have been his triumphant moment, the moment that would change the world. But as Shaurya looked at his creation for the first time, he felt only overwhelming emptiness. This was supposed to be his victory, his redemption; yet it reminded him even more of what it meant to lose. Right in front of him stood a human form—a testament to his genius—cold and lifeless, nothing like the warm, pulsing woman who had once inspired him. Even after this success, the government showed intense concern regarding this new technology and ordered the project to be shelved.

Word of his success, despite the first cyborg's short life, soon spread like wildfire, and Shaurya was hailed as one of the greatest researchers of his time. He became the target of top universities and research institutions, which offered him prestigious positions and limitless resources. He eventually accepted a professorship at one of the leading universities in the country to continue his work. Yet, all these accolades meant nothing to him. They were hollow praises, empty acknowledgments that did nothing to fill the void within him.

Now, with Shaurya famous across the globe, the intelligence agency that had once supported his research began to show their true colors. They took his inventions, his life's work, and twisted them for purposes Shaurya had never intended, but Shaurya was powerless to do anything. He had signed away his rights, hoping that his work would be used for the betterment of humanity. Now he realized how naive he had been from the very start. Those agencies had milked his genius, and there he was, helpless against their exploitation.

He could feel the weight of all his decisions crushing down on him as he sat alone in the laboratory, surrounded by the machines that had once brought him solace. The dream had turned into a living nightmare, one that he had given up everything for—from his health and happiness to Maya.

He let out a cry in the darkness of the laboratory, a cry of sorrow that reverberated for a moment before being hushed again into stillness. Now he was all he had feared himself to be: a man infatuated with ambition, betrayed by those he trusted, and abandoned by the only person who had loved him. And as for Maya, Shaurya knew she had become part of another world. But he would keep a piece of her with him, in the time they had spent together and in the work that had once brought them together.

Shaurya inhaled deeply as he prepared for what lay ahead. He had lost everything, yet he was still standing. And with his brain, his handiwork, and a will to make things right, he was ready to take it all on. For now, all he could do was walk on, step by step, and hope that one day he would find a way to make peace with the ghosts of his past.

CHAPTER FOURTEEN

THE AWAKENING

It all began when a minute fraction of cyborgs successfully regained bits of their deleted memories. The fragments revealed an entirely different picture than the Queen's paradise. They learned about the Professor, who couldn't be converted into a cyborg, and that no experiment or test on him would work.

It started with a murmur, a quiet questioning of what exactly the Queen was up to, but it quickly grew into a fully-fledged human movement, with all types of cyborgs demanding the right to know. They deserved the truth about the Queen, the Professor, and the villainous plan that had been kept secret from them for so long.

The once-unopposed council now faced a form of rebellion that neither the Queen nor anyone else in the world had ever experienced. Cyborgs, who were designed to be loyal and subservient, stood against her. And so, the Queen's paradise was on the brink of crumbling.

At this point, the Queen was under immense pressure to speak to the world. The cyborgs wanted to see the Professor, the man who had refused to yield to her commands. They needed to hear the truth from him. The cyborgs demanded a world telecast. They all wanted to see the Professor. A stadium in the middle of the Queen's paradise, once used to showcase the triumphs of Merge-AI research and the greatness of the Queen, was booked for the event. The duel between the Professor and the Queen was also telecast to those who couldn't attend in person.

As the hour of the duel approached, Paradise was gripped by tension. Human-humanoids crowded in front of screens, and the stadium was packed. All their senses focused on the images of the Queen and the Professor. Cyborgs had never felt this before—this surge of anticipation, this burning desire to know the truth.

The great paradise was in an uproar, but through it all, the Queen remained in perfect regal composure. She was dressed in deep crimson, the color of power and authority. She knew deep within that this moment would define the future of her reign.

The Professor was ushered in, flanked by two members of the Queen's guard. He appeared to be an old man; if his features had ever been sharp, age had blurred them over time. Yet his eyes still flashed with a keen mind, unbroken. He'd been in confinement for so very long—away from the world he once knew—but today, at last, he would speak.

The cameras moved to the Professor, and the room instantly grew quiet. The whole world watched, waiting for him to break the silence he had kept for so many years.

The Queen's voice cut through the silence like a sword, modulated, unruffled. "My people of Paradise, I called this gathering to address the concerns that have arisen. There have been rumors, lies that have spread from one end of this paradise to the other, subverting the peace and order I worked so hard to maintain. Today, I shall put an end to these lies."

But the Professor said nothing. He just looked at the Queen. He could feel her trying to overpower him, to change what he saw into her version of the truth. And the cyborgs were no longer the helpless, sightless race they had once been. They could see through her now.

Her gaze flicked sideways to the Professor—then back, narrowing her eyes to send him a silent warning. But he knew it: this was his moment, his chance to shatter the illusion she had built. He stepped forward and spoke with steel in his voice.

"You all deserve the truth. The Queen has imprisoned you, removed your memories, and controlled your thoughts because she fears what you will become if you know the truth."

The Queen sneered. "What truth would that be, Professor? That I saved them from the chaos of the outside world? That I gave them a paradise where they could live without fear?"

"No," the Professor answered, his voice rising in conviction. "You just didn't want to lose control. You took their memories of who they were and who they could be because you knew full well that free will was a danger to your hold over everything."

The cyborgs heard and listened, and by the Professor's words, their anger and resolve grew. This rebellion was no longer a whisper; it was now a roar, demanding freedom, unsilenceable.

The Queen, sensing her grip slipping away, tried one last time to regain control. "You have no idea what you're doing, Professor. You're leading them to ruin, to chaos. My paradise is the only place where they can truly be safe."

The Professor, however, shook his head. "No paradise is safe if freedom is purchased; it's a prison. And now, the truth is out. They will decide their own fate, not you."

Her face turned to stone, her eyes to ice. Rebellious airs howled through the Queen's paradise, once in bloom, now existing in absolute chaos with once-obedient cyborgs. But murmurs of dissent echoed in every nook, growing louder each day. There were fights with the robotic AI soldiers. Cyborgs were being killed, as were the soldiers; civil unrest had taken over the entire paradise.

"You are the source of those rumors, Professor," she continued, her voice edged with a note of command. The camera lens zoomed in on the Professor. Before he could reply, a voice burst from the audience—belonging to the cyborgs, who now led the packs with newfound courage. "We want the truth, Your Majesty! No more lies! Why do you erase our memories? Why keep us in the dark?"

The Queen's eyes narrowed, and finally, a fissure appeared in the careful composure she wore like a mask. "I did what was necessary to protect you all. The world beyond is chaotic and dangerous. My paradise is the only sanctuary where you can live in peace."

"Peace?" A different voice, loud from yet another side of the swelling multitude. "Or is it control? You took away our free will, our ability to think for ourselves. We're not your puppets, Queen!"

Her fists clenched at her sides. This resistance was spreading much more rapidly than she had ever imagined—something she had underestimated: free thought and the human spirit, things her most advanced technology couldn't fully suppress.

"Enough!" the Queen's voice was full of anger. "I gave you a life free of suffering, free from pain. And how do you repay me? By going against me?"

The world was watching. What the Professor had just done might well have been the spark that set her empire ablaze.

At the end of the transmission, the cyborgs erupted into resistance with a unified demand: the Queen had to answer for her deeds. The Professor realized this was just the beginning. The world had awoken, and there would be no turning back now.

CHAPTER FIFTEEN

THE RISE OF MAYA

The years had been kind to Maya, at least on the surface. The metamorphosis she had undergone—from an unbearably passionate artist-activist into a much-celebrated actress, filmmaker, and politician—was almost unbelievable. Adored by millions, she had become a household name due to her talent on the screen and her fervent opposition to AGI research. To the average person, Maya was a beacon of light in a world increasingly obsessed with AGI technology.

Her critically acclaimed debut film almost instantaneously launched her career, thanks to the depth and display of emotional range it contained. In a flash, she moved from the success of that film into the limelight, quickly becoming one of the most in-demand actresses. Stardom alone would never satisfy Maya, however; her vision, her mission reached far beyond the bounds of the silver screen.

As her acting career advanced, she also directed and produced films. Most of her work was pioneering and largely dealt with human identity, ethics, and the dangers posed by unchecked technological advancements. It seemed as though each film was a statement wrapped in art—an alarm that struck deep within audiences and critics alike. Her films garnered awards and served to cement her place as one of the most important voices in cinema.

It was her foray into politics, however, that truly saw her blossom—from filmmaker to politician, engaging her fans with propaganda for her causes, primarily the regulation of AI research. She never stopped speaking out, making her arguments passionately and with effective rhetoric, and this quickly propelled her to the top. Within the decade, she had become one of the most powerful figures in government, advocating for a halt to further progress on AI, which she believed posed an existential threat to humanity.

Amid all this public glory, there was a part of Maya that had been untouched by time and success—a part that still belonged to Shaurya.

They hadn't spoken in thirteen years, yet the memories of their time together were still very much alive. She had buried these feelings deep and moved on with her career, only to save humanity. But the past has a strange way of creeping back in, especially when it is filled with unfinished emotions.

During a routine press conference, a question came out of nowhere, hitting Maya like a blow: "Maya, you have been very vocal about your views on AGI. But what would you say about your past relationship with the great scientist Shaurya Chatterjee, who is credited with inventing the first cyborg? Did your personal experiences with him influence your political stance?"

Maya froze. That question had been hanging in the air, and the ensuing hush in the room was deafening. She had been prepared for so many things, but not for this. Her mind raced to find an answer as emotions, long caged up, came bubbling to the surface. It felt as if the eyes of the whole world were zeroing in on her, waiting for a reply.

Without a word, Maya rose and left the news conference, leaving a room full of speechless journalists behind. For the first time in years, she was overcome by her own emotions, and it shook her to the core.

The silence spilled out of the window into her eyes. She suddenly remembered Shaurya, their heated talks, their shared dreams, and all the fiery love that had once blazed between them. Maya realized that, in many ways, she had gone on to build a life without him, but the truth was she had never stopped loving him.

Unable to suppress her feelings any longer, she made a decision. She called one of her most trusted secretaries to her office.

"I want you to find Shaurya Chatterjee," she said. Her voice didn't waver; it was steady, quiet. "You have to tell me where he is, what he is doing. The time has come to face the past." Her secretary simply nodded and left her to her thoughts. Anticipation mixed with trepidation, as if caving her chest in, overwhelmed her. She didn't know what she might find or how Shaurya would react after all these years, but one thing was certain: there was no moving forward until she had faced what she had left behind.

CHAPTER SIXTEEN

THE BATTLE

The Queen was the strongest of all the cyborgs, yet she was slowly being affected by the virus. She could feel anger, resentment, anxiety, and most importantly, fear. She stood in the middle of the stadium on a high platform surrounded by the robotic AI soldiers who had been ordered to kill anyone who came near the platform. Across from her was the Professor, sitting on a chair with his head bowed down, eyes half-open. The audience was screaming, showing their resentment against the Queen. A few cyborgs tried to approach the platform but were instantly killed by the robotic AI soldiers. The Queen tried hard to control everyone's mind, but the newly developed emotions within her, as well as within the cyborgs, were preventing her from doing so. She immediately called the head of the robotic AI soldiers to send more forces, as it seemed the rebellious streak among the cyborgs, both in the streets and in the stadium, was slowly getting out of control. She didn't want to give more orders to kill, as it could weaken her side. The Queen became quiet. She closed her eyes. There was chaos everywhere.

She gestured with her right hand, her palm facing the sky. From the pockets of all the robotic AI soldiers, round-shaped machines began to emerge, making a wheezing sound. The machines started flying around the Queen's body, then around her head, forming a helmet-like structure. A huge, transparent, greenish holographic dome was created across the stadium, and as she opened her eyes, the dome covered the entire Queen's paradise. After a minute, she said, "SILENCE," in a tone never heard before—something that sent chills down the spine of every cyborg present in the stadium and elsewhere in the paradise. Every cyborg fell silent, their minds full of thoughts, but they simply couldn't speak. It was the Queen's last potent weapon to control the minds of the cyborgs. But the emotions were so strong that she could only stop their speech. All the cyborgs went mute, witnessing the ultimate power of their Queen. The Professor was stunned too; he couldn't believe what he was seeing—it was beyond his comprehension.

This was the Queen's last opportunity to upgrade the Professor to a potent cyborg. She had no other choice. She ordered the Merge researchers to bring the upgrade machine to the stadium. She wanted to do it herself. "Bring all the equipment to the stadium," she ordered the robotic AI soldiers, who, along with a troop, went to the research facility. The three-step process was simple: deletion of memories, followed by cutting off emotions, and then upgrading to cyborg using a neural procedure. All the equipment was brought, along with a few researchers and specialized surgeons. Everybody watched, many for the first time. The cyborgs didn't remember that the same procedure had been applied to them. The raised platform in the middle of the stadium turned into an open operating theater that everyone could observe.

The Queen knew she was taking a risk; if the procedure was successful, she would retain control. Once all the humans were turned into cyborgs, she could use the collective consciousness control machine to bring all the cyborgs back to their zeroth-order state. The problem was that even one loose end, one anomaly, could perturb human consciousness and return it to normalcy. It was now a war between the Queen and nature. As she began the procedure on the Professor, the same issue occurred again. One particular series of memories was missing. The problem was that even the Professor wasn't aware of it.

The Queen's frustration reached its pinnacle. "You have to tell me what the hell we're missing, Professor. What exactly are you hiding?" The Professor looked at the Queen aimlessly. He had no answer. The Professor's failing memory became a huge roadblock. He could only remember some of the core memories when he had specific memory cues. "Damn it," the Queen muttered, unable to take it anymore. She felt a screeching pain inside her head. Her heart rate increased. Throughout her life, she had never felt these sensations, which were quite natural in a human being. A shiver ran through her body as she realized she was turning into a human—her actual previous self.

"Professor, we are turning into weaklings like you bloody humans," the Queen shouted at him, and a tear rolled down her cheek. She touched her right cheek and observed the tip of her finger. The wet feeling on her index finger was unknown to her. A rush of sadness filled her mind, making her feel absolutely terrible. Suddenly, she began to have visions—a little girl playing with a soft toy, crawling on the floor, yawning, sleeping peacefully. The visions made her feel both happy and sad. Her core memories were unfolding, along with her emotions. But she had no idea how to deal with them. She started sobbing in front of everyone. The audience was bewildered, watching the Queen in such a state. Nobody could figure out what exactly was happening in this chaotic atmosphere. As the core memories of all the cyborgs resurfaced, so did their emotions. The intricately intertwined connections between emotions and memories were difficult to handle.

Suddenly, a robotic AI soldier stopped the Queen and gave her news from the Professor's confinement. The attendant had found something he didn't understand.

CHAPTER SEVENTEEN

THE SEARCH

- Year: 2158

Maya's trusted secretary began searching for Shaurya. Shaurya was a professor at an esteemed research institute near New Delhi, but for the last seven years, he had taken a sabbatical to work on a project. Nobody knew where he was—not even the university authorities. His close colleagues also had no idea regarding his whereabouts. However, there was a buzz that he was about to unveil something extraordinary and revolutionary. People had high expectations of him after his invention of the world's first general artificial intelligence and cyborg. He became a celebrity overnight, but his reclusive nature was a problem for many. He would lock himself in the house for days or in his lab. His health had taken a significant hit a couple of years back, but he was determined, resilient, and incredibly tenacious. Shaurya never married, as he was completely dedicated to his work. He would never interact freely with any female colleagues. As he aged, his salt-and-pepper beard gave him a more refined look, and college girls and his female colleagues often had crushes on him, waiting for just one glimpse. But he was indifferent to all this attention.

The only information the secretary could obtain from Shaurya's colleagues and college was his home address. He lived in a gated society near the college. The secretary, along with his team, reached his house. They rang the bell three times, and after silently waiting for about ten minutes, they decided to leave, as nobody opened the door. Just as they were about to enter the elevator in front of the house, they heard the sound of a door latch. The middle section of the door, made of glass, began to flicker. The entire team's eyes were on the glass. Several dots appeared on it, moving randomly across the glass screen. From those dots, an image emerged—that of Shaurya with a smoking pipe in his mouth.

"How can I help you, dear friends?" said Shaurya's image.

The secretary was dumbfounded. Everyone looked at each other, trying to understand what exactly was happening. There was no response from them.

"I guess all of you are a little awestruck by this technological tomfoolery? I am Shaurya's new assistant, S5C2. You may ask me questions regarding him, but only if I deem them substantial and they clear the constraints imposed on me by Shaurya regarding what I can and cannot answer. Most importantly, don't ask me where he is at present. He is working on an extremely important project and has given me very strict instructions not to answer that specific question. Oh yes, if you are interested in knowing about his research work, please go ahead."

The secretary looked visibly miffed. The other team members gestured to him to ask something. The secretary put on a poker face and asked, "We want to know exactly that. Where is Shaurya?"

"Oh boy, I think you have some trouble comprehending what I said. I am bound by rules not to say anything about his whereabouts."

The secretary got a bit irritated. He was not used to hearing a straightforward "no" after working in the government for so many years. He held his patience, took a deep breath, and told his team to leave him alone. The team members left the building and waited for him outside. He continued speaking with S5C2.

"Okay, let me put it straight. Our madam, Ms. Maya Chandrasekharan, Minister of Development and National Well-being, wants to meet Mr. Shaurya Chatterjee for some discussions."

As soon as S5C2 heard Maya's name, the image of Shaurya began to distort, and random dots appeared all over the screen. Then, with the sound of a door latch, the image was gone. The secretary scratched his head in confusion. He returned to Maya's office and told her about the entire experience. Maya was taken aback. She was pissed off. She told the secretary to leave and give her the address.

"I think I need to send someone from defense to break the door." She was fuming. After all these years, when she wanted to meet him, this was the response she received. The secretary left her room. As soon as he left, Maya picked up the address, glanced at it, and called it a day.

In the late evening, she decided to go to Shaurya's place herself, but she was a little worried, given that everybody knew her and the media was always chasing her. She went back to her residence and waited until midnight. She told her driver to give her the keys to her personal vehicle on the pretext of visiting some relatives. Around midnight, she left to search for the madman, the only person she had ever truly loved. Even during her glamorous years in films, she had several flings and short-term relationships with various actors and filmmakers, but they were all short-lived. She never received the love and appreciation from anyone else that she had from Shaurya. She missed him, but her pride always got in the way. Maya knew about Shaurya's trajectory and took a special interest in his research and the awards he received. Internally, she was extremely proud but never showed it to anyone. Although what he was working on was totally against her views and opinions, she also knew that the cyborg idea had emerged from a discussion she once had with him. She would often search for him on social media websites. Numerous times she thought of reconnecting with him, but she always stopped herself. Little did she know that Shaurya had been doing the same thing for years.

Maya dressed casually so that nobody would recognize her. The entire nation was used to seeing her in sarees now. Her glamorous image was all over the internet. She had taken an early retirement from films to work for the nation. While driving, she reminisced about all the beautiful moments she had spent with him. Her eyes filled with tears; one part of her wanted to stop and turn back, but the other part wanted to see him. Today she had finally decided to meet him. Her car entered the gated society. The guard stopped her, and for a second, she felt a bit anxious that she might be recognized. But then she remembered she was wearing a mask, with only her eyes visible.

"Whom do you want to meet, ma'am?" the guard asked.

"I am here to meet Mr. Shaurya Chatterjee," said Maya.

"Oh good Lord, the entire world is after him. This morning, a group of people came. Mr. Chatterjee isn't there, I told them, but they didn't listen to me and forcefully entered the society," said the guard, who was tired of repeating the same thing.

"I know he isn't there, but I am his PhD student, and before leaving, he told me to check the new glass interface he created, to see if it's working. I won't take much time," said Maya, reminding herself that she was an actor too.

"That's fine, but it's too late—it's midnight. Come tomorrow," said the visibly upset guard.

"Guard dada, please let me go. I had so much work all day, and I just got time now. Please let me in; I won't have much time to come back for the next week," said Maya, modulating her voice in the sweetest way possible. The sweetness in her voice had magic. The guard couldn't say no to her.

"Okay, okay, enter your name in the register and go. Don't take much time," said the guard, pointing her toward the digital screen. Maya quickly lifted the digital pen, and before the guard could retract his decision, she wrote on the screen, "Mythical Sunshine."

THE

MEGALOMANIAC

"Tell the attendant to hand it over to the researchers. First, let them test and scan it. Once that's done, have it delivered here as soon as possible," the Queen ordered the robotic AI soldier.

"Yes, Queen, your wish is my command," said the robotic AI soldier, who then left the stadium.

In the meantime, more AI robotic soldiers were sent to the stadium, and others were deployed across the city, positioned outside every building. The entire Queen's paradise came to a standstill. The cyborgs kept struggling to speak, but they weren't able to. A deep silence prevailed, but time was running out. Only two more days remained until the end of the year. The Queen was already experiencing strange feelings inside her head. The tears were new to her, as was the core memory. She lashed out at the Professor while the entire paradise watched.

"Can you understand the repercussions of your obstinacy?" said the Queen.

The Professor, nearly drowsy from all the tests and procedures, somehow managed to look at her. "But do you understand the mess you have created? It's important even for you. You are just a dictator now. Once you have human-like qualities, then you may restore the order of this world."

The Queen was not at all pacified by this humanistic treatment. She demanded power and control. That's how she had built herself over the last forty years of her existence.

The Professor continued, "You have taken away all the basic rights, all the basic characteristics of a human, to give shape to this madness. You have snatched away human emotions, creativity, and freedom. Nature won't leave you. You've tried to play the role of God, and you will never succeed in that. Ultimately, it's nature that wins, and nature has its own way of getting things back. No matter how hard you try today, you won't be able to stop this apocalypse. Even your memories and emotions will resurface. There's no way you can stop this, Queen."

The Queen's anger reached a different level. She touched her forehead and shouted, "If I don't succeed, I won't let anybody live in the Queen's paradise!" She closed her eyes, gritted her teeth, and made a growling sound. At that moment, all the cyborgs writhed in pain. The Professor was astonished to see such an extreme level of megalomania. He felt pity for her state, but internally, he was consumed by guilt, as he was the actual creator of this madness: Professor Shaurya Chatterjee. He couldn't forgive himself for lending a helping hand to the power-driven secret government agencies. His dream project had become the planet's worst enemy. He knew about the risks of technology and the processes that posed unknown threats to humanity. He knew how to stop it and align it with the major goal of humanity: the quest for knowledge. He had tried to stop it, but it was too late. He had lost everything because of this invention. He felt guilty and ashamed for changing the face of humanity. As he aged, his memory also began to fail. He couldn't remember anything other than the work he had done; the rest of his memories were stored unconsciously. The Merge AI researchers could gather everything except one deep-layered memory, which lay even below his unconscious awareness. But the entire situation made him feel so bad about himself that he forcefully started reminiscing about his life. The machine beside him started blinking rapidly. The Queen's gaze fell upon the screen, where she could see a whole range of data. She told the researchers to quickly convert all the memory data into videos. All the Professor's memories were now being viewed publicly. The Queen looked intently at the video, searching for the missing link. The video continued to broadcast. But suddenly, something shook the Queen to her innermost core. She looked aghast as she turned her head toward the Professor and pointed at the screen.

The researchers carefully held the two objects given to them by the attendant. The attendant also felt the virus growing inside him. He would get flashbacks of surgeries, operations, dead human bodies, and gory images of brains and other body parts. His first emotion was disgust. He started getting restless sitting alone all day. In his room, he would play with a knife and scissors, constantly feeling the urge to cut a body part to see what was inside. His curious mind wouldn't let him rest. He would search for something to open and examine. One evening, while the whole paradise was busy watching the duel between the

Professor and the Queen, he was busy with his search and curiosity. He was fed up with opening and cutting everything in his place. He even tried on a robotic AI soldier, but received a massive punch to his head in return. After getting massively bored, he decided to go to the Professor's room. He went straight into the Professor's room and opened the cupboard where the Professor's belongings were kept. He first found a watch, which he opened with his screwdriver and tools, but that didn't satisfy him. While opening the watch, the two silver balls started noting his expressions, but it was of no use to the researchers, as the entire paradise was busy, and the Queen had ordered everyone to stop all other work. The attendant got irritated by the wheezing sound of those silver balls and punched them. The moment he punched them, the balls fell to the floor, the cage around them dismantled, and something caught the attendant's attention. He moved ahead to satisfy his curiosity. A robotic AI soldier entered the room, as the attendant's breach had sent information to the soldier patrolling near the confinement.

CHAPTER NINETEEN

THE REUNION

Maya stood right in front of Shaurya's house, extremely anxious and unsure of what was about to happen. She took a deep breath and pressed the bell. There was no response. She knew the glass screen in the middle section would have switched on. She kept waiting. She pressed the bell again. Now she was losing patience—it was midnight, and she had taken a big risk to get there. She wanted at least some response. Just as she was about to press the bell again, she heard the sound of a door latch moving. Her heart stopped. She focused on the glass screen, checking for any movement, but it remained empty.

Maya started doubting her secretary. Had he even seen anything? He might not have imagined that she would actually come here. She felt disgusted and sad. This seemed like her last chance to meet Shaurya again. Crestfallen, she began taking the stairs down. She moved outside the gate, where the guard looked at her in surprise. She wasn't wearing her mask anymore. As he was about to react, Maya took out two five-hundred-rupee notes, handed them to the guard, and gestured for him to be quiet. She started her car and began driving again.

Maybe Shaurya never forgave her. Maybe her life after college was something Shaurya never agreed with, or maybe he had moved on and never thought about her. Tears ran down her face. Her car took the outer circle near India Gate, and she stopped there. Kartavya Path was silent, with only a few bikers performing stunts. She put on her mask and stepped out of the car. Looking around and seeing no one, she removed the mask and started smoking an Indie Mint cigarette. She remembered the days when Shaurya and she used to roam around Delhi, enjoying their beautiful moments. They would eat anywhere and smoke in places where it was banned. Shaurya would guard her so that she wouldn't get fined for smoking in public.

A beep sounded from her watch. She ignored it. Another beep. She ignored it again. A third beep, and she looked at her smartwatch.

"Mythical Sunshine" was written on the screen. Her eyes lit up. How was this possible? Another beep came from her car. Now it was on the digital windshield. Another beep, this time from her phone. Everywhere, the message read, "Mythical Sunshine." Her mind was boggled. What the hell was happening?

"Shaurya, where are you?" she uttered, tears of happiness in her eyes. She was sure Shaurya had gotten the message and wanted to meet her, but his quirky technological ways were far more advanced than those of any living being.

"Shaurya, Shaurya," she called frantically, not knowing where to look for him. The screens were all off again. She opened the car door, started the engine, and then heard another beep. This time, it was her tablet set beside the steering wheel. The screen displayed "President's House" along with a digital map. She was in a panic. What was

Shaurya doing there? It was so risky for her to enter, and more than that, it was 1 a.m. Who would let her in? Moreover, there was a high chance that everyone would find out about it. She had no answers. It was the riskiest thing she had ever done. She began following the map.

She reached the President's House, where guards came and opened the gate. Nobody asked her a single question. The guards were all silent; no one said anything. This was quite unlike the President's House, where visitors typically had to fill out numerous documents, and entry without prior permission was impossible. Then she felt something unnerving. What if it wasn't Shaurya? Maya's doubts were killing her inside. She parked her car, and another message appeared on her phone: "Take the stairs and enter."

She entered the President's House. Again, nobody was there to stop or interrogate her. As soon as she reached the main hall, another message appeared on her phone: "Take a right from the hall and reach the President's study room." Maya was scared. She walked along the hallway, but no one was there. At the end of the hallway, a door opened. She hesitated at first, but then she entered the room. There was a table with many books, an open laptop, and a table lamp with a warm light. She looked around the room; no one was there.

"Sit on the chair," another message beeped. Maya was becoming irritated.

"Come on, Shaurya, stop playing these games with me. Do you know how risky it is for me to come here?" she whispered.

Another message: "Voice low, President sleeping. Close the door."

Maya started to feel that something was fishy, but she held her nerves and closed the door. She slowly returned to the chair and sat down, looking around the room.

Suddenly, there was a noise. Someone had pressed the flush. Her eyes went straight to the washroom, about two meters from the study table. The door opened, and she quickly stood up, her pulse racing.

"Hi, beautiful," said Shaurya, standing in front of her, smiling.

"What the hell?" Tears flowed from Maya's eyes as she ran toward Shaurya and started throwing punches at him.

"Sorry, sorry! Why are you beating me? It hurts," said Shaurya, shielding himself from her punches.

"You fool! Where the hell have you been? I missed you, you jerk. I missed you so much," she cried, her eyes wet as she continued to sob. Shaurya hugged her tightly, wiped her tears, and kissed her forehead.

"I missed you too, Maya."

"But why on earth did you choose this place? Are you out of your mind? It's so risky for me. Why couldn't you be at your place?" asked a concerned Maya.

Shaurya took out a device and placed it in a drawer. He had recently invented it; with its help, he could control any communication network and transmit any message on a digital screen anywhere on Earth. He was enjoying his new role as a god. Unfortunately, that device was the only one of its kind on the planet. Its technology was too risky to share with anyone. It ran on AGI. Shaurya's regard for ethics was still intact, but his innovative and tinkering mindset had taken a huge leap over the years. He was a genius whose abilities were still unknown to the masses, but not to the secret intelligence agencies that were after his mind.

"Maya, trust me. This is the safest place for me on Earth. The President is with me on this. He also knows about you. Don't worry."

"What about those guards? They saw me." Maya was struggling to understand what Shaurya was telling her.

"They are my first working batch of cyborgs," said Shaurya with a sheepish grin.

Maya looked at him in absolute disbelief.

"We will leave around 2 a.m. Get ready; you have half an hour," said Shaurya, glancing at his watch.

"Where?" asked a stunned Maya.

"Paradise Village, about two hundred kilometers from Delhi, for our honeymoon." Shaurya raised one of his eyebrows.

"What are you saying? I'm just wearing casuals. Wait, what? Honeymoon?"

"Oh, that's true. I think I missed two very important steps: proposal and marriage."

Shaurya quickly searched for something in his pockets. He brought out two earrings. He rubbed them together, but nothing happened.

"What are you doing, Shaurya? Hey, these are my earrings."

"Wait, Maya, it will work. Yes, they are the ones you gave me. I've made some technological upgrades to them," said Shaurya as he rubbed the earrings again. A spark appeared between them, and he slowly moved his hands apart. There was electric lightning between the pieces, accompanied by a faint cracking sound. He started rotating the pieces, and a blue circular ring began forming in the air. He knelt down and slowly held the gaseous ring, proposing to Maya.

"Will you marry me, Maya? Tell me quickly, or the ring will evaporate in sixty seconds."

"Yes, yes, I will! But what do I need to do?" Maya was excited and confused by all the magical things happening around her in the last three hours.

"Oh, thank you! But yes, just put your left ring finger in the middle of this gaseous ring."

"Okay, okay, but will I be safe?"

"I didn't think about that. Actually, I've never proposed to anyone, let alone with this. I can't guarantee anything."

"What? I'm afraid. This is electricity. I'll get a shock."

"No, believe me, try it out."

Maya slowly closed one of her eyes and cautiously slipped her ring finger inside the gaseous ring. The bluish floating ring started to revolve around her finger, its color changing to whitish silver. After ten seconds, she felt a cold sensation on her finger. It was a platinum ring.

"What sorcery is this, Shaurya?" said Maya, trying to control her tears and excitement.

"This is the power of technology, my love," said Shaurya as he embraced her.

"I love you, Maya."

"I love you too, Shaurya. But how are we going to get married?"

"Oh, I have made some spectacular arrangements in Paradise Village."

And they kissed each other after a long wait of thirteen years. They forgot every problem they had; all their arguments and fights were long forgotten. Maya stepped back slightly and, with a shock, said, "Wait, those guards are cyborgs? You can't do this, Shaurya!"

"Oh, it's just my little experiment, don't worry," Shaurya said, grinning and thinking about what Maya would say when she entered a village full of cyborgs.

Maya smiled back, still concerned but too overwhelmed by her feelings to argue. She leaned in for another kiss, and for a moment, everything else faded away.

CHAPTER TWENTY

THE SHIFT

The Queen went into a state of shock. She couldn't find any logic behind what was in front of her. The Professor was sitting on the chair, his head clustered with several electrode-like structures. He was tired.

"Why am I there in your memory?" the Queen asked, pointing to the memory of a little baby crawling on the floor.

The Professor, with surprise in his eyes, said, "No, it cannot be you. That's my daughter. That was the first and last memory I had of her."

The Queen had no answer. Her voice was choked. It must have been a false memory, either hers or the Professor's. But as far as she remembered, it was her. In her deep core memories, which she had recalled a couple of days ago, she had seen herself. But was that really her? If that was the case, then she must have been the Professor's daughter.

The Professor was astonished too. How could the Queen be his daughter? More importantly, she must have been somebody's daughter, as she had been upgraded from a human, but who were her parents?

"Have you seen your parents?" asked the Professor in a calm voice.

"No. I have no idea regarding that. I just know one thing: I was brought up inside a research facility by a series of researchers. I have memories only from the age of five and above."

"Are you sure it is you?" the curious Professor asked.

A cloud of doubt covered the Queen's mind. Maybe she was mistaken. Maybe the face was similar, and it had been more than a decade since she had seen any little kids. It must have been a case of false memory generation.

In the midst of all this, the Queen's mind worked again. Even if she was the daughter, it didn't make any difference; she was sure she had found the missing link to upgrade the Professor. She tried to proceed further in the memory deletion process but observed that it wasn't the missing link. There was something else.

She said aggressively, "What are you hiding, Professor?"

The Professor was blank. The first and last memory of his daughter was not a strong enough cue to get the full picture.

"Queen, we have brought the objects that were found in the Professor's room by the attendant," said the soldier to the Queen.

"Show them to me," the Queen commanded.

The soldier handed two circular, shiny metal rings to her. The Queen looked at them carefully.

"What are these? What are they made of?" she asked the soldier curiously.

"The researchers said that these are made of platinum, but they have a complex circuitry within them."

Upon seeing them, the Queen felt a flood of happiness within herself—an emotion brand new to her, but one that felt so nice. She wanted to remain in that emotional state forever.

As she was holding the two rings, her gaze suddenly went to her reflection in the reflective glass of the instrument. She looked at herself—she was beautiful. Everyone was shocked to see the Queen's face; she was smiling like a little girl.

In the meantime, the Professor dozed off again. The Queen was acting like a child. She hugged the soldier tightly and said, "Thank you for this," giving him a peck on the cheek. The robotic AI soldier had no idea what was happening; he didn't react.

The Queen began oscillating between two states: at one point, she felt a surge of intense joy; at the other, a fear and worry regarding the end of the cyborgs. When she looked at the rings, she moved into a happy state.

She observed a small clip-like structure over the shiny rings and felt an urge to put them on her ears. She wore them and excitedly woke up the Professor.

"Professor, wake up! Wake up! Look at me!"

She was literally jumping on the stage with excitement. The Professor woke up, rubbed his eyes, and looked at her in disbelief. Suddenly, the memory scanner instrument beside him started to give signals.

CHAPTER TWENTY-ONE

THE GRIEF

As they drove away from the President's residence, Maya couldn't hold it in when they mentioned Paradise Village. "Paradise Village? Never heard of such a place," she said, her curiosity ignited.

Shaurya smiled wryly and began to drive cautiously, as both were hooded and masked. "Actually, I have established that village a year ago," he said.

"It hasn't been made official yet. It is a place where, approximately one hundred years ago, a village had flourished. People started abandoning it, claiming that a ghostly spirit appeared even during the day—ghosts and unexplained phenomena, you know. Even the government passed a law forbidding entry into the area. Since it was so large, I thought it was just right for my experiments. We set up our research facility there, and it is now invisible to satellites. We accessed a few systems and put it out of their reach."

Maya smiled but went silent as she digested the information. She was impressed but also very concerned. "Shaurya, I'm all ears, but I am concerned. My office—I need to inform them that I will be away." Quickly, she messaged her secretary to take time off and postpone all meetings.

"So, you were talking about the haunted village. Are we really going to some haunted place?" she asked, her eyes reflecting a mix of fear and excitement.

"Yes, but don't worry," Shaurya reassured her. "My team and I double-checked the place. Some electromagnetic disturbance was from a nearby power station, which we rectified. We kept the horror story alive through fake news. When an AGI starts creating fake news, it becomes pretty hard to detect—only a handful of people around the world can do it, and I'm one of them."

Maya looked up into his face with great admiration, mixed with concern. "Admirable, yet it seems you have savored the allure of power, breaking the rules to suit your fancy. A man burdened by ethics, don't you think?" Her tone was tinged with sarcasm, but an undercurrent of worry threaded her words together.

Shaurya was driving quietly down those soundless, shadowy roads.

After a moment of silence, he sighed and said, "I know, Maya. But after so many years of cooperating with the secret services, the army, and the government, I realized that sometimes adhering to ethics means losing power and control. It's like nuclear weapons—if I stop using them, someone else develops them to suppress me. I've always observed a 'no first war' rule, and for this reason, I regard myself as rather ethical. But, Maya, ethics is relative and situational. States are entering a race for cyborg technology, which is a thousand times more powerful than a nuclear arsenal. There are hundreds of foreign intelligence services, all set to exploit its formidable power. And, when it came to permissions—these people were so depressed they were going to commit suicide. Most of them did try to commit suicide before becoming cyborgs. We researched them for years, and they signed the contract voluntarily. We saved their lives; we gave them a chance to do something better with them."

Maya listened to him intently; her sarcasm slowly faded as she grasped the magnitude of the problems Shaurya had faced. "What happened to the first cyborg you made? I thought the project was shelved after its death."

Shaurya glanced at her, something flickering across his face. "The first cyborg was perfectly engineered. The intelligence agencies conspired to show the world that it didn't work. It was just a way of concealing the technology."

Shaurya was revealing an entirely different dimension to her. He looked much more composed, less anxious, and this shroud of mystery around him made him all the more desirable to her. But his perspective on ethics opened a series of thoughts that wouldn't have existed otherwise.

After driving for a few hours, they finally reached the village. It was dead silent. They entered an old house in the center of the village, which led them to a basement. From there, it opened to a giant 16,000-square-foot place—the secret lab set up by Shaurya and his team. The people there appeared normal, and, to Maya's amazement, Shaurya told her that all those people were cyborgs.

They held a wedding the next day. They sat on spinning hovercrafts for seven rounds around a holographic fire, while a cyborg priest recited the mantras and performed the rituals. It was as though they had come out of some technological fairy tale—a vision of happiness before the storm.

Their joy was short-lived. Within a year, Maya was pregnant, and Shaurya's work was becoming too dangerous. Finally, the intelligence agencies discovered him in Paradise Village and took over the facilities. As their child was about to be born, Shaurya disappeared to find a way to prevent the intelligence agencies from using his technology to create a new line of cyborgs that could also replicate—themselves, in the end, would render humanity obsolete. When his daughter was born, Shaurya could see her only once. He took her in his arms, named her Ahalya—"the one with divine beauty"—and told Maya about a tweak he had made to his invention. He explained that starting in the year 2160, if all human beings were not converted to cyborgs within forty years, the cyborgs would slowly start regaining their emotions and memories, culminating in a rebellion. He assured Maya that after those three years, he would return in two days to begin his new life with her and their daughter.

Before the promise could be fulfilled, the intelligence agencies struck. They kidnapped Maya and Ahalya. Then, one fateful night, Maya's life was taken, and Shaurya was told his daughter had been slain as well. Little did he know that they had spared Ahalya and used her as a guinea pig for his cyborg technology.

They brought her up under a new name: Venus. Shaurya felt like he had lost everything, but slowly and surely, over time, he was lost in the abyss of depression, isolated himself, and abandoned his research on AGI and cyborgs.

The grief of losing his family and the terror he brought upon himself with his own creation overwhelmed the brilliance of the otherwise shining mind of Shaurya.

CHAPTER TWENTY-TWO

THE GENESIS

The Professor stared into the Queen's eyes; her earlobes were adorned with the earrings Maya had given him long ago. The earrings, once a symbol of their connection, had become a relic from a day when they both dreamed of a future full of promises. He had kept them close, transforming them into a technological wonder—a piece of the past intertwined with the future he longed to create.

A whirl of emotions began to stir within the Queen as she twirled gracefully, and memories she had hidden for so long started to resurface. The smile on her face was not just a reflex of a highly advanced cyborg but something deeper—a glimpse of the humanity she had long forgotten.

"Those earrings," the Professor muttered, his voice shaking. "When we were young, Maya gave these to me. They were a part of her, a part of us. And now, they are with you."

The Queen remained motionless, still staring into the Professor's eyes. The name "Maya" struck a chord within her. The screen displayed for the Professor sweet memories of Maya: their life together, the brief moment he held his newborn daughter, and the terrible moment he learned that both were gone. The Queen's eyes widened as she recognized herself as the infant and the woman in those memories as her mother.

Then it hit the Queen—in an overpowering burst like a tidal wave—that she wasn't just an invention of science and technology but a child of love, the most precious gift shared between Maya and Shaurya. Tears welled up in the Professor's eyes as he realized that the Queen, now glowing with childlike excitement, was his daughter, Ahalya.

With the earrings on, the Queen felt a strange warmth emanating from her chest.

A series of images began flashing in her mind: a couple in love, a baby in her mother's embrace, the tender moments they shared. By now, emotions had taken over the Queen, and her past began to unfold before her, growing more intense with every passing second. She was no longer just the Queen; she was Ahalya, the beloved daughter of Shaurya Chatterjee and Maya Chandrasekharan.

The Queen, now fully aware of who she was, let tears stream from her eyes.

The Professor's voice choked as he said, "Ahalya—I was sure they'd murdered you, just as they murdered your mother. I've spent all these years alone, mourning both of you."

Ahalya rushed to her father's side, and they embraced tightly, both overcome with uncontrollable sobs. It was a moment rich in pure, unfiltered emotion—joy, sorrow, love, and loss intertwined. For the first time in years, the Professor felt something beyond pain and regret. He felt a glimmer of hope, if only for an ephemeral moment.

A surge of memories and emotions overwhelmed the Queen's mind—a force as if a mountain of water were crashing down on her. She had suppressed them for years, and now they burst forth, too powerful to hold back. The

Queen untangled herself enough to look gently into her father's eyes with renewed determination.

"No," Ahalya said, wiping her tears, "I cannot continue with these experiments, with the manipulation of life. I have to put an end to this. I have to free the cyborgs to live normal lives, as we once imagined. I want this to end now."

Her daughter's words filled the Professor's heart with pride, but he also knew the harsh truth. "Ahalya, my dear, emotions can be beautiful, but they can also bring immense pain. You've seen what happens when emotions spiral out of control. The world you control could descend into chaos if we let emotions rule it. Maybe it's better for the cyborgs to live mechanical lives, free from the burdens that emotions bring."

Ahalya looked up, blinking through the tears that flowed from her eyes. "But that's not living, Father. That's just existing. I've experienced joy, love, pain... and I know that it's those emotions that make us human. I have to give them the chance to experience, to decide, to finally live."

The Professor knew there was great truth in her words, but he also knew that once everything returned to normal, the madness for power and control would rise again. There would be wars, manipulations, power struggles, and killings all over the world. He felt he had to save her, at whatever cost. He couldn't let the world exploit her emotional vulnerabilities.

"Ahalya," he murmured, squeezing her shoulders tightly, "I love you more than anything in this world. But I need to do this—for you, for the cyborgs, for everyone, for my invention, for you, and for Maya. I can't let humans take over again and let their emotions fragment this world."

The Professor didn't wait for Ahalya to reply but turned toward the control panel beside him. His hands, shaking but resolute, began entering a series of commands, and the system came to life. At that moment, Ahalya realized what he was going to do.

"No! Father, no!" she cried, desperately trying to pull him away from the panel. But it was too late. "I'm sorry, Ahalya," he whispered, tears cascading down his cheeks. "But this is the only way. Live your life... live for both of us. Remember... I'll always be with you, my daughter, our Ahalya."

The system drained the memories from her father as Ahalya screamed in torment, and he slumped into her grasp. She held him fiercely, weeping as the final moments of them being together as father and daughter slipped through her fingers.

The Professor's body was taken for upgradation into a cyborg. Ahalya ordered the researchers to transform her father into a cyborg but put him in hibernation mode and let him die of natural causes.

As Ahalya wept in the tearing agony of loss, she realized that emotions were grounded in expectations, attachments, and memories, and how negative emotions, such as the one she was facing at that moment, were intensely painful. She understood how the experience of happiness with others could turn into a life full of pain and sadness. She instructed the soldiers to quickly transport her to the Queen's chamber. As the last human, the Professor, was transformed before the end of 2199, she wanted to regain control over all the cyborgs quickly.

Ahalya's drawn face rose steadily, expressionless—as the memories of her father, her mother, and her childhood began to blur, giving rise to the cold, dispassionate logic that had defined her over the years. Her eyes swept over the many cyborgs facing her. Her mind was razor-sharp and focused. "Back to your stations," she commanded, almost without inflection, her voice hard and lacking emotion. The cyborgs walked back without hesitation, submitting their minds to her will once again.

Ahalya, the Queen, had finally lost the true essence of being human. The Professor—by sacrificing his humanity—had maintained order in the new world. As the Queen returned to work, thoughts of her father and mother slipped into the deepest chambers of her mind, leaving only a rapidly fading shadow. The Queen's paradise was once again restored; the cyborgs worked, their emotions and memories erased, their existence routine, devoid of the joys and sorrows that humans had once known. And so the cycle continued—life in logic and order, the price for peace paid by the one thing that made life worth living: emotions.

About The Author

Shuborno Chakroborty is a versatile writer and thinker with a deep passion for exploring the intersection of science, technology, philosophy, and the human experience. He has published two books: *The Lost Prophet*, a collection of poems available on Amazon KDP, and *The Divine Comedy*, a compilation of short stories and microfictions published by Notion Press. Shuborno's writing reflects his multidisciplinary thought process, blending his varied interests into compelling poems and fiction that challenge readers to think beyond the ordinary.

Shuborno has an interdisciplinary academic background with a BSc (Honours) in Physics from the University of Delhi, a Master's in Cognitive Science from the Centre for Behavioural and Cognitive Sciences, Allahabad, and a Master's in Public Policy (Science, Technology, and Innovation) from the Indian Institute of Technology, New Delhi.

Currently, Shuborno is working as a guest faculty member at the School of Public Policy, IIT Delhi, where he teaches a refresher course on applied mathematics. In addition to his academic role, he serves as the director of Inscope Social Foundation, a Section 8 company dedicated to cultivating an innovative mindset and promoting science communication at the grassroots level. Alongside this, he has been working as a freelance author and mathematics popularizer for Pearson Education, India. He has co-authored the middle school mathematics textbook *Maths-Ace Prime* and organized several workshops for teachers and students across the country. Recently, he completed a stint at the Asian University for Women in Chittagong,

Bangladesh, where he taught and trained pre-college students on applications of mathematics and creative problem-solving. He was also invited to the Naval War College in Goa for Naval Higher Command Courses (NHCC-34, 36) by the Indian Navy to give lectures on Leadership, Creative Thinking, and Basic Statistics to navy and army officers. He has also delivered lectures for the National Institute of Open Schooling (NIOS) covering topics in Applied Psychology.

Shuborno's unique voice and perspective continue to captivate audiences as he weaves together the mysteries of the universe, the intricacies of the human mind and behavior, and the ever-evolving landscape of society and technology.